John Bedford Leno

Drury Lane Llyrics

And Other Poems. Second Edition

John Bedford Leno

Drury Lane Llyrics
And Other Poems. Second Edition

ISBN/EAN: 9783744777308

Printed in Europe, USA, Canada, Australia, Japan

Cover: Foto ©Andreas Hilbeck / pixelio.de

More available books at **www.hansebooks.com**

DRURY LANE LYRICS,

And other Poems.

BY JOHN BEDFORD LENO.

[SECOND EDITION.]

LONDON:

PUBLISHED BY THE AUTHOR, 56, DRURY LANE,

AND SOLD BY ALL BOOKSELLERS.

1868.

56, Drury Lane, London,

December, 1867.

It is a time-worn custom when an author presents a volume to the public, to offer a few prefatory remarks. Let me candidly confess that, while I believe in this custom, I find great difficulty in saying aught that would either excuse the deficiencies or increase the value of what I have written. The fact of publishing is in itself a confession that I believe my verses are not absolutely worthless, but this belief may result from the greenness of the spectacles through which authors are too apt to view their own productions.

My readers will, therefore, accept this as an apology for declining a task for which I feel a certain degree of incompetency, and leaving the results of my labours, with this slight preliminary bow, to the unbiased criticism of a free press, and the generous consideration of an indulgent public.

TO THE

TOILERS OF ALL NATIONS,

THIS VOLUME

IS RESPECTFULLY DEDICATED BY

THE AUTHOR.

CONTENTS.

CONTENTS.

DRURY LANE LYRICS.

THE TRAVELLERS.

I.

I saw a traveller passing o'er a bleak and barren heath ;
    I said, " Where art thou roaming,
    And crowds that now are coming ? "
He answered, " To the gorgeous home of Death ! "

II.

His locks, that had been raven, were white as driven snow ;
    His frame, that told the story
    Of wasted strength and glory,
  Was bending, 'neath a heavy weight of woe.

III.

I pointed to a stone, and bade him rest awhile.

 I knew that he was weary—

 The way both dark and dreary :

He shook his head—and answered with a smile :

IV.

" I have rested far too long in this dismal vale of tears :

 No comfort can I borrow

 From such a land of sorrow,

Although I've been a dweller four score years !

V.

" The world tells me I'm travelling to a bleak and friendless

   shore—

 But every friend I own

 Is going—or has gone—

So let me tread the path they trod before !"

VI.

He journeyed on his way, and others passed along—

 The young and old together—

 No resting place for either ;

I could not weep for all—so wept the young.

VII.

So silently they passed—like a noiseless breath of wind :
 Some hearts were wrung with anguish,
 While others seemed to languish
For treasures they were leaving far behind !

VIII.

But one whose bright eyes sparkled—who travelled
 on alone ;
 Whose brow was so benignant—
 It seemed that naught malignant
Had ever sat there—rested on the stone.

IX.

" From all that's gay and lovely, 'tis soon, alas, to part ;
 To rove through scenes of gladness
 In solitude and sadness,
 Before the warmth of youth has left my heart.

X.

" I journey to a land where all is dark and gloom :
 I trod the maze of pleasure,
 And thought to find a treasure,
And when I thought I'd found it—grasped a tomb !

XI.

" Beware! my friend!" he said, " even Pleasure is unkind :
  She sends you on a journey,
  And like a shrewd attorney,
Keeps each treasure of your untaught youth behind."

XII.

He passed, and left me standing more a sage than I had
    been ;
  I saw that Death and Terror
  Were only linked by Error :
I saw the world as Youth and Age had seen.

XIII.

You pass along a valley, and at first you see but flowers :
  You gather them in wonder,
  Until you hear the thunder,
That, bursting, tells of coming storms and showers.

XIV.

In vain you search for shelter, where no shelter's to be
    found ;
  The rain—the storm is blinding ;
  No flower—no heart's-ease finding—
No more you see the beauty spread around.

XV.

And he that gathers largest of the flowers he may find,

    Will leave this world's plethora,

    As Lot's wife left Gomorrah,

And often cast a lingering look behind!

WILD FLOWERS.

I.

As we rambled through the meadows
On a sunny Sabbath morn,
The church-bells ringing merrily, so merrily;
With a nosegay white with meadowsweet
And blossoms from the thorn,
We laughed and chatted cheerily, cheerily.
'Twas a nosegay of wild flowers,
I remember it quite well,
With its daisies from the uplands,
And its cinquefoil from the dell,
With its yarrow, ling and larkspur,
And the little pimpernel,
Gathered while the bells rang merrily, so merrily! so
merrily!
Gathered while the bells rang merrily!
So merry, merrily!

II.

We have plucked a many nosegays
Since that sunny Sabbath morn,
When the church-bells rang so merrily, so merrily!

And we've made them white with meadowsweet
And blossoms from the thorn,
And laughed and chatted cheerily, cheerily !
But that nosegay of wild flowers
Is before my vision still,
With its wildlings from the hedgerow,
And its daisies from the hill,
And the yellow daffodillies,
Freshly gathered from the rill,
While church-bells rang so merrily, so merrily ! so
merrily !
Gathered while the bells rang merrily !
So merry, merrily !

.

III.

Come along my pretty maiden,
'Tis a sunny Sabbath morn,
The church-bells ringing merrily, so merrily !
Let us wander through the meadows,
Till we reach the trysting thorn,
Where lovers linger cheerily, cheerily !
I remember well each flower,
Let us gather it again,—
The crowfoot from the marshland
And the mallow from the plain ;

The wild thyme from the little copse,
The bluebell from the lane,
While the church-bells ring? so merrily, so merrily, so
merrily!
While the church-bells ring? so merrily!
So merry, merrily

———————

THE CROWDED COURT.

I.

As I gazed from out my window on the crowded court below,
Where the sunshine seldom enters and the winds but seldom
     blow,
I behold a flow'ret dying for the want of light and air,
And I said, " How fares it, brothers, with the human flow'rets
     there ? "

II.

By and by I saw a little hand stretched through a broken
     pane,
" I have brought thee," cried a little voice, "a cupful of
     God's rain ; "
But rain alone would not suffice to raise its drooping stem,
And I thought of those who dwelt below and longed to suc-
     cour them.

III.

On the morrow, ere the noontide, as I wandered down the
     court,
Through a brood of little children, flushed alone by ruddy
     sport,

I drew a little girl aside and bade her tell to me
The name of those who dwelt within the cottage numbered
      three.

IV.

With little bright eyes sparkling through her flaxen, un-
      kempt hair,
She answered, " I will tell you ; there are many living there!"
And swiftly with her nimble tongue she ran the whole list
      through,
I gave the child a penny, and she curtseyed and withdrew.

V.

Let those on mercy's errands bent be never turned away !
There was fever raging all around those children in their
      play ;
And in the little stifling room, outstretched upon the bed,
The sister hands to that I saw were lying cold and dead.

VI.

I called the flow'ret's friend to me, and kissed her pallid brow ;
I longed to bear her far away, where healthful breezes blow;
She told her tale of heartfelt grief as innocence can tell ;
I never heard a tale so sad in sorrow told so well.

VII.

Toll, toll the bell! another and another has been slain!

No more shall I behold that hand stretched through the
shattered pane!

They bear her to a sunny spot, where flowers bud and bloom—

The spot that should have been her home is chosen for her
tomb!

VIII.

But what of those yet left behind within that sunless court?

Shall they be left till Death shall come and end their child-
ish sport?

And she with flaxen, unkempt hair, with bright eyes all
a glow—

Shall she, like others, perish in the crowded court below?

THE RIVALS.

I.

THE stream o'er the pebbles was singing a song,
    And its burthen, its burthen was love ;
And he sang it so merrily, sang it so cheerily,
    To a leaf gaily dancing above.
The stream sang so merrily, early and late,
    Never tired of singing, of singing, was he,
Thou can'st ride on my bosom, where many a blossom
    Has rode like a queen to the sea.

II.

The flowers had passed from the shores of the stream,
    When the north wind came lashing its tide,
And the rival was young, and the rival was strong,
    And he bore off the leaf for a bride.
And he sang a rude song as he bore her away,
    A rude song of triumph, of triumph, sang he ;
Thou shalt ride on my bosom, where many a blossom
    Has rode like a queen to the sea.

III.

Over high towering mountains he bore her away,

    Not a span from the portal of heaven ;

Over deep tangled glen and the thronged haunts of men,

    She rode from the dawn till the even :

And he sang a rude song as he bore her away,

    A rude song of triumph, of triumph, sang he ;

When she fell from his breast from a towering crest,

    And was caught in the lap o' th' sea.

THE INVITATION.

I.

Oh, come where streams are singing, and meek-eyed flowers
    springing,
  And catch the breezy freshness of the morn ;
Come, come to yonder meadows, as night calls back her
    shadows,
  And hear the lark's soft twitter 'mid the corn ;
Then mark his flight so high, proudly soaring to the sky,
  And listen to his matchless flood of song ;
List! list its wondrous sweetness, then mark th' appalling
    fleetness
  With which it bears Heaven's message to its young.

II.

Oh, come where fruit trees swelter in the sun, and ask no
    shelter—
  Save that which heaven above them e'er bestows ;
Oh, come where myriad flowers win new life from the shower,
  And all pay adulation to the rose

Where the meek forget-me-not is contented with its lot,
  And the violet, retiring from the crowd,
Breathes prayers so sweet and holy—so humble and so lowly—
  Each breathing checks the arrogant and proud.

III.

Oh, come where wild-fowl gather, and bathe each silken
      feather
  In the deep and placid waters of the lake ;
Where the Suicide, unholy, rushed from life and melancholy
  In the undisturbéd silence of the brake ;
Where the guilty Maniac stood, with his hot hands bathed in
      blood,
  And tell me, is there aught to favour crime ?
Is the bulrush by its border an emblem of disorder
  That proudly shuns contagion with the slime ?

IV.

With wonder and emotion, come view the bounding ocean,
  And seek for hidden life within its caves ;
And place beyond conjecture earth's hidden architecture—
  The wonders of the cauldron of the waves ;
Come view each magic cell where nymphs of ocean dwell,
  And tell me, is there aught on earth more grand ?

Stay wild waves on their passage, and learn th' important
      message
  With which they run like coursers to the land.

v.

Come, list to nature's vesper—the soft and silent whisper
  Of branches as they rock their babes to rest;
And tell me the revealing of subtle thought and feeling
  That stirs the hidden pulses of thy breast;
Oh, tell me what they say—be their story sad or gay,
  I would that nature's secrets were revealed,—
A leaf's most gentle flutter, doth some precious wisdom
      utter
  That since creation's birthday has been sealed.

VI.

Cease, cease your vain repining, and come where stars
      are shining,
  And view the glitt'ring crown above your head;
And tell me where each cluster of stars begets its lustre—
  By whom the mighty hosts of Heaven are fed!
Then turn your eyes to earth, and talk of drought and dearth,
  And dismal tales from lands beyond the sea;
Of nations torn asunder by kings, who live to plunder,
  And trample out the life-blood of the free.

VII.

Come, come, with all your learning, your well-conned book-
        lots spurning,
    And read a single leaf of nature's page ;
Come, come, and read the story of all earth's wondrous glory,
    If thou wouldst be the prophet of the age ;
For there alone thou'lt find the loadstone of the mind,
    The power to draw its hidden treasure forth,
Come back, come back to Nature, she'll give thee thy full
        stature,
    And thou shalt guide the children of the earth.

VIII.

Come, tell me, tell me fairly, divinely and sincerely,
    Hast thou beheld a single sign of care?
Where'er thou found'st a blossom with tears within its
        bosom,
    Pray, tell me, was no rainbow shining there ?
Come, tell me, why it is—while all is bathed in bliss,
    And flowers grow untented side by side—
That man, divinely gifted, from happiness has drifted,
    Unmindful of the current and the tide ?

IX.

    Oh, tell me why he fritters his time in culling bitters,
    When precious fruit hangs tempting o'er his way !

Or why, whene'er he rambles, he wanders 'midst the brambles
    To grasp the Dead Sea apple of Dismay?
Has Wisdom but began to shed her light o'er man,
    That, like the blind, he only feels the light?
Is God's divinest creature redeemless in each feature,
    And doomed to be a foe or anchorite?

X.

Is every hope's revealing, that, o'er my senses stealing,
    Lets in more glorious sunshine from above,
A figment or delusion, creating vain confusion—
    A mockery of universal love?
It cannot, cannot be, when all I hear and see
    Repeats the glorious promise made and sealed!
It cometh soon or later, all God's great mediator,
    To living man and woman has revealed.

XI.

It cometh in the burning east-born sun that lights the morning,
    On heaven-directed flashes of the night;
It rides upon the shadowy cloud that skims the meadow,
    And nought but daring madness stays its flight;
It leaves the home of malice, it shuns the tyrant's palace,
    It quits the home of sin where madmen rave;
And over to the nation that gives its slaves salvation,
    It rideth on the white crest of the wave.

SONG OF THE SPADE.

I.

Give me the spade, and the man who can use it ;
  A fig for your Lord and his soft silken hand ;
Let the man who has strength never stoop to abuse it,
  Give it back to the giver—the land, boys, the land.
There's no bank like the earth to deposit your labour,
  The more you deposit, the more you shall have ;
If there's more than you want you can give to your neigh-
    bour,
  And your name shall be dear to the true and the brave.

II.

Give me the spade ! England's hope, England's glory !
  That fashioned the field from the bleak barren moor.
Let us blazon its rare deeds in ballad and story,
  While 'tis brightened with labour—not tarnished with
    gore.
It was not the sword that won our best battle,—
  Created our commerce—extended our trade,—
Gave food to our loving wives, children, and cattle,—
  But the queen of all weapons—the spade, boys, the spade.

III.

Give me the spade ! there's a magic about it
   That turns the black soil into bright shining gold ;
What would our fathers have done, boys, without it,—
   When the lands lay all bare, and the night winds blew cold?
Where the tall forest stood, and the wild beasts were yelling,
   And our stout-hearted ancestors shrank back afraid,—
The rich corn-stack is raised, and man claims a dwelling,
    Then hurrah ! for our true friend—the spade, boys, the
      spade!

THE CAVALCADE.

I.

Long I sat and watched it passing,—
   'Twas a mighty cavalcade,
Flushed with daring deeds of valour,
   Throwing former deeds in shade.
They had proved to be the stronger
   Of the nations of the earth—
And their valour shed a glory
   On the land that gave them birth ;
But I dare not call them conquerors,
   They were proud, too proud, for men ;
And the wise should e'er be wary,
   E're they praise the weak and vain.
So I let the throng pass onward,
   Till their tramp was heard no more,
And I straightway fell a thinking,
   Of the many who were poor.

II.

There were little children starving,
   None were toiling for them now ;

They were weak in mind and spirit—
  Famine sat upon their brow!
They had learned to steal so early
  That their first crime was forgot:
They had prayed for food and mercy,
  But the rich had heard them not:
They had told their sad tale often,
  And each true heart could but bleed;
But the false hearts are so many,
  And the true so few indeed:
So I sat myself a thinking,
  When their tramp was heard no more,
And my heart was near a breaking
  For the many who were poor.

III.

There were some whose names were branded
  For the crimes their fathers wrought,
But who bravely struggle onward
  'Gainst the tide of ill report.
Though the strong may reach the haven,
  Dashing wave on wave aside;
There are thousands doomed to perish
  Overpowered by the tide.

How their piercing cries go upward
  You may learn if you but hark—
How they sink beneath the ocean,
  How they die out in the dark !
And my heart was near a breaking,
  When their tramp was heard no more,
And I prayed for heaven to shield them,
  And to save the many poor.

IV.

There were mothers cursed by children,
  Whom they bravely bore in pain—
And they called to God in anguish
  " Take them, take them back again ! "
Women forced to part with virtue,
  Dearer to them than blood ;
And brave women too among them,
  Who the fiery ordeal stood.
There were brave hearts filled with anguish
  There were faces pale with woe ;
There was many a weary traveller
  With a weary way to go.
And I prayed that heaven might shield them,
  When their tramp was heard no more :
And my heart was near a breaking
  For the many who were poor.

V.

There were others rich and wealthy,
   There were many boasting ease—
Decked with gay and gaudy trappings,
   That assorted ill with these.
And I said, " If such be conquerors,
   Then let flatterers call them so—
For the trappings and the trimmings
   Will not heal the heart of woe.
Let the cavalcade pass forward,
   While the wise look on and see—
How a nation crownéd conqueror,
   May have won but misery.
While I sit me down and fathom,
   Now their tramp is heard no more,
How the good may change to blessings
   All the ills that men endure."

KING LABOUR.

I.

THE wizard, King Labour, walked over the land,
   And the spade for a sceptre he bore ;
And each step he took left an Eden behind,
   While the desert untamed frowned before.
He levelled huge mountains, and blasted the rock,
   Where for ages vast treasures lay hid,
And shewed Heaven the coffer where Earth stored her wealth,
   And laughed loud as he shattered the lid.
Then shout, toilers, shout, we need no king on earth,
   But the king whose large, generous hand,
Has scattered bright gold over mountain and plain,
   And whose taxes are wrung from the land.

II.

I marked every step the magic king took,
   Till he bounded the wide spreading plain,
And I marked how the eye of God followed his path,
   While the heavens sang a gladsome refrain.

And this was its burthen—" There's plenty for all,
  Look abroad in the light of the day,
And view the corn challenge the sickle and scythe,
  With its lances well poised for the fray."

III.

The harvest well garnered—Toil's heralds went forth,
  Their speed by Good-Humour increased,
And they said to each child of the universe, " Come !
  And let none be shut out from the feast ! "
" Come, come," said King Labour, "Earth's treasures are mine,
  Bid the tyrants of earth to beware ;
Their bride may be Death, if they court Famine's hand,
  For still there's the Sword of Despair ! "

LOOK UP.

I.

Yon castle's strong as iron bands,
  But heaven above is stronger;
The castle's stood a thousand years,
  But heaven has stood much longer ;
The castle is the work of man,
  The proudest and the strongest;
The blue heaven is our God's old work
  And made to last the longest.
                    Look up—look up !

II.

Fear not the castle's sullen frown,
  Though hoary turrets linger—
They long have felt the touch of time,
  Bear impress of his finger ;
But heaven, eternal heaven, above,
  The birthright.of the humble,
Supported by Almighty God,
  Will strengthen as they crumble.
                    Look up—look up !

III.

No talo of woo to blanch the check
　Is heard in heaven—no sorrow
Comes tripping on tho heel to-day
　To stand at bay to-morrow ;
No agonising foars strike dumb,
　No grief produces blindness ;
But white-winged angels hover round,
　And whisper words of kindness.
　　　　　　　Look up—look up !

IV.

Within tho castle on yon hill,
　Abroad in yonder valley,
In gold bedizened palaces,
　In street, and lane, and alley—
Grief leaves its traco on every brow,
　A canker in each bosom,
Which kills the red roso on the check
　Ero it can bud and blossom.
　　　　　　　Look up—look up !

V.

Beyond tho snow-clad mountain brow
　The sun is brightly shining,

Amid the fadeless hues of heaven
  The soul knows no repining ;
And through the mists that crown the hill,
  Where endless clouds upgather,
A voice comes ringing in mine ear,
  The voice of God the Father,

      " Look up — look up ! "

SONG OF THE SLOPWORKER.

I.

For twenty summers I've sat and toiled,
　　Buried alive in this fever den ;
Ay, toiling, toiling, ever toiling,
　　To clothe my wealthier fellow-men !
I've seen no field, no thorn, nor flower,
　　From its parent sod up-springing ;
No leaf-clad bough, no rain-bowed sky,
　　Nor "lark at heaven's gate singing."

II.

Scarce forty years, and these hairs turned grey,
　　Scarce forty years, and my manhood fled !
And yet, 'tis strange I've lived so long
　　On poisoned air and tear-steeped bread !
'Tis strange, indeed, I've not sought Death,
　　But stranger he never found me ;
When he has feasted by my side,
　　And conquered all around me !

III.

I've sat and toiled in this prison-room,
    Till all around was dark and drear ;
Ay, clothing Idleness in velvet,
    While I had scarce a rag to wear.
I've had no man to call me friend,
    Nor soul to soothe my sorrow !
A desert bounds my view to day,
    A sea of ice to-morrow !

IV.

For twenty years, in this garret high,
    I've lived alone 'mid a million souls ;
Passing along the road of life,
    And doing nought but paying tolls.
I've crossed no earthly paradise,
    No chequering spots of gladness,
And every finger-post was marked
    " To Suffering " and " To Sadness."

V

Wedded to pale-featured Poverty,
    She ruled my fate with an iron hand !

And every structure I sought to raise
  Was built by hope, and based on sand!
Each dream of my youth has passed away,
  All craving for life been banished;
And I cry to my God with upraised hands,
  "Is there hope, when all hope has vanished?"

WORDS OF HOPE.

—

I.

I NEVER turn me backward,
 To mark the road I've trod,
But I feel Hope's dews fall on me,
 And a firmer faith in God ;
I hear an angel whisper,
 " Wait ! wait a little while ;
Time's wand shall touch the cold world's frown
 And change it to a smile ! "

II.

I've passed the darkest morning
 That ever fell on man ;
But never, wearying, faltered,
 Since earthly trials began ;
I felt the stars were rising,
 And saw with inward ken,
A future, big with promise,
 Dawn on happier, wiser men.

III.

The wisest of Earth's children,—
  The great among the great,—
In the long Cimmerian midnight,
  Foretold a New Estate:
Saw unborn golden ages
  With far, out-reaching mind,
And died to seal their advent
  And the freedom of mankind.

IV.

'Tis strange that aught in nature
  Should ever know despair;
It cannot look around it
  And read God's writing there;
It cannot heed the teachings
  Of the star-bejewelled skies,
Or it would know that hate and wrath
  Are untaught sympathies.

V

I have seen the mind's misgiving
  When Grief lay anchored there;
And marked the flagging footstep
  Of mortals bowed by care:

But brave men will to conquer
   When cowards shun the fight ;
Hence none should fear the issue,
   Whose soul yearns for the right.

———————

RABBIE BURNS.

I.

The Robin that sung by the ploughrail
    Was missing one fine summer morn ;
And the kind mate that wooed him and won him
    Sighed deeply her Robin's return :
But the city her lost one had flown to
    Had few charms for the bird of the grove,
And, disgusted, the brown-coated Robin
    Flew back to his home and his love.

II.

The cage that enticed him was golden,
    The food was both tasteful and rare ;
But the bird loved the wildwood and freedom,
    Though the trees were quite fruitless and bare :
And 'twas well that gay Robin flew homeward,
    Ere robbed of his eyesight for song ;
Or the bird that sung loudly for Freedom
    May blindly have flattered the Wrong.

A FRAGMENT.

I.

A DESPERATE game—a sudden, fearless fate!
  'Twere better far than shaking hands with Death;
Or walking to the tomb with Grief, disconsolate—
  The sword long rusted in its narrow sheath.

II.

Give me the blast of war; no peaceful reed:
  The blood-stained corslet to the wedding gown;
Exchange the lamb for some stern warrior steed—
  A smiling death is but a gilded frown.

III.

Living, at best, is action—labour—strife!
  And he who crowds the most in one short space,
Alone can taste the richer wine of life,
  And view the grave a well-won resting place.

IV.

Who worthier than the labourer ? who so lost ?
  Ignored by parasites, and pimps, and spies ?
His blood extracted by a soulless host,
  He lives on sufferance, and, despairing, dies.

V.

God of my fathers ! shall it aye remain ?
  And truckling Peace be courted for her glance ?
Eternal sunshine desolates the plain ;
  Eternal truces check the soul's advance.

VI.

The stagnant lake is covered o'er with slime,
  And such are nations with their filth a-top :
With Wrong triumphant, Peace is but a crime
  That runs like bindweed over Virtue's crop.

VII.

Methinks I see a bloody carnival
  Ere hard-hand Labour shall preside once more ;
When arméd hovel dares the gilded hall,
  And drives its inmates to Hell's blackest shore.

VIII.

There is no health in quiet ; howling storms,
 And rude and untamed thunder are the springs
Of life, and if in death we fatten worms,
 On earth, at least, we will not toil for kings.

FAIR CHILD OF THE SUMMER.

I.

Fair child of the Summer, and miniature test
   Of the delicate pencil of Nature,
Was ever such art in an atom expressed,
   As in thee, thou ephemeral creature?
Thou wooer of flowers and symbol of soul,
   Thy life is too short to be wasted;
Go, sip the rich nectar of each floral bowl
   Thy butterfly lips have not tasted.
Kiss the marginal flowers that garland the spring,
   Wake the lily asleep on the river,
Ere the mildew shall fall on thy beautiful wing,
   And its brightness be tarnished for ever.

II.

Spread thy gossamer wings to the bright summer skies,
   Ere the noontide shall fade in the gloaming,
For jealousy lurks in a thousand bright eyes
   That long have kept watch on thy coming:

The reddest of roses are paling with woe,
  The day's-eyes (*) with anguish run over:
And the poppy that grew in the trail of the plough,
  Is hiding its grief in the clover.
Kiss the marginal flowers that garland the spring,
  Wake the lily asleep on the river,
Ere the mildew shall fall on thy beautiful wing,
  And its brightness be tarnished for ever.

(*) Daisies.

ECLOGUE.

Hail! Brother of the Plough! hast any news?

Not I, in faith, since poor Tim Bobbin died;
And then 'twas sorry news: I used to think
'Twas time the earth was flooded once again.

Much good it did, that flooding of the world:
'Twould seem as though fair Virtue had been drowned,
And Vice alone e'er reached Mount Ararat,
As worthless scum will ever float a-top!
But I have news, if thou wilt lend thine ear.

There is no scholar in the village now
To read the news before the ale-house fire,
As Tim was wont on every Sabbath eve—
(God rest in heaven his wearied, honest soul!)
So I have ears to lend thee for thy news.

STRANGER.

The North long slept, as any child might sleep,
Unmindful of the chains fell tyrants forge ;
Or like to Samson in Delilah's arms,
Who woke to find his every limb enslaved ;
But this is past, and never more to be :
The tide of time has baffled charms and chains,
And Samson has regained his pristine strength.

RUSTIC.

I have no ears for riddles such as thine,
Whose sense entangled leads my mind astray !
Are poor men ever likely to be free ?
Are masters born with less than stony hearts ?

STRANGER.

The poor man's freedom lies within his grasp ;
To sting him if he falter at the touch,
To bless him if he grasp it with his might !
The hardened heart is but the coward heart,
Steeped in the changeful waters of success,
Till flesh and blood are changed to nerveless stone.

RUSTIC.

Like thee, Poor Tim would oft forget his woes,
And tell strange truths in stranger words than thine.

STRANGER.

Would he were living, though, perhaps, more blest,
His spirit dwelleth on a calmer shore,
That ho with you might listen to mo now,
While I relate a wondrous miracle !
A mighty prophet, moving through the north,
Has stirr'd a pulse that throbs from shore to shore,
And poor men gather up their scatter'd strength,
Within the tether of a mighty wrong.
He walks amid those cities of the north,
More like to God than aught of human kind!

RUSTIC.

Thy news is like an echo to mine cars,
An echo of an ardent prophecy
That Tim would make while reading of fell wrongs.

STRANGER.

Ay, so it may ; for many have foretold
That Poverty would one day raise its voice,
And cry aloud for Justice to be king.
His words when utter'd find a full response
In all who listen to his truth-fraught tongue ;
And cities, like the glorious stars of night,
Burst through the darkness of a thousand years,
And throw a radiance over all the land.

Maids, mothers, and their little ones are free,
And leave the pent-up chambers of their woe,
And bless their God (for so they do believe)
For sending a deliverance from toil
More fatal than the bondage Egypt bore.
The very hills seem loftier than they were!
The valleys breathe an incense still more sweet !
The trees in adoration bow their heads !
And rivers murmur songs of boundless joy !
Come, leave thy toil, the tidings shall be known
From sea to sea, till all this mighty world
Shall sing a song of universal joy.

ELLEN RAY.

I.

A BLITHE and bonny, winsome lass
 Was Ellen Ray, dear Ellen Ray;
But youth and beauty quickly pass,
 Like summer flowers, away.
Her cheeks were red, her hair was brown,
When first she came to our town;
But now, alas, all beauty's flown
   From winsome Ellen Ray.

II.

I asked if she would be my bride,
 Dear Ellen Ray, dear Ellen Ray;
Her bright eye, lit with maiden pride,
 Spoke more than tongue could say.
From that glad hour, in storm and strife,
We've clung, as though a single life
Alone was ours,—and still my wife
   Is winsome Ellen Ray.

III.

But though all beauty long has fled
   From Ellen Ray, dear Ellen Ray,
Her beauty other beauty fed
   That fills my sight to-day.
The loveliness that Time despoiled,
The beauty that in Ellen smiled,
Has found a refuge in the child
      Of winsome Ellen Ray.

A STREET REVERIE.

I.

WHERE was thy blushing girlhood passed?
  'Mid fields of fragrant flowers?
Where maiden faces brighten with tears,
  Refreshing as April showers,
And where thy heart ne'er knew the grief
  That conquers and overpowers?

II.

I know not; yet I fain would bring
  Lost treasures to thy mind,
In hopes thy torn and bleeding heart
  Some comfort thus might find;
For I have sometimes comfort found
  In comfort left behind.

III.

I cannot tell the giant grasp
  Such fates have won o'er me;

But once I saw a fated barque
　Upon a troubled sea,
And still I see it hurrying on
　Whene'er I look on thee.

IV.

There thousands hurried to the beach,
　Uncivilized were they :
Here thousands watch the vessel sink,
　And none e'er step astray :
" The wreck has oft been plundered,"
　Their carnal souls do say.

V.

And what do I but pity her ?
　Should I chance step aside,
I blush if man should recognise
　Me standing by her side,
And then I curse my coward heart,
　The refuge of all pride.

VI.

When sinners turn to their sinless days,
　The smouldering spark will glow,

And the blackest heart that man could own
　　Is whiter than drifted snow,
And the brand of Cain, indelible,
　　But dimly marks his brow.

SEEKING THE SPRING.

I.

STRIKE again, strike again ! every well-planted blow
Brings you nearer, still nearer, to water below ;
All the lands lying round us are famished and bare,
There's a plague in the sunshine, and death strides the air.
The rich spring has long slept in the cavern confined,
And the land has been kissed by the hot burning wind :
'Till the children who blessed her have withered away
In the morning of life, and the glory of day.

II.

When the prophet of old struck the strong mountain side,
The swift waters came rushing forth glad as a bride,
And those throbbing beneath you shall burst through their cell,
Crown the mountain with verdure, and clothe the nude dell.
Ply away, ply away ! there is life in each stroke,
'Till the doors of the prison are shattered and broke,
'Till the grim tyrant Death, as he rides through the air,
Sees his form in a mirror, and flies in despair.

III.

Strike again, strike again ! you have unchained the stream—
See, it rises up now, like a child from a dream ;
And the earth laughs to scorn the young maid's modest sip,
As she drains a brave tankard with fever-parched lip.
Now, behold the old toper grows merry once more,
As she feels a new life—with fresh hope for the poor,
And Death's powerful grasp is unnerved by dismay,
As the stream, like a blind girl, goes feeling its way.

AN ADDRESS TO WINTER.

I.

Thou'rt coming once again : I hear thee speak,
In no mild mood, upon the mountain side :
And from the shore, where ceaseless surges break,
I see thee seated on the crested tide.

II.

I know thou'rt coming, for I saw the sun
Weep tears of pity for her children fair ;
The trees are stripped for fight, and streamlets run
Without a ripple, as though swoll'n with care.

III.

I saw the housewife bind the unused door,
And marked the sadness seated on her brow,
While lab'ring hard to make each seam secure
Against thy bitter warriors, Frost and Snow :

IV.

I heard the north wind whistle as it passed,
　　As though 'twas heralding a conqueror's train ;
While, o'er the earth, a spotless robe was cast,
　　And forests grew upon my window pane.

V.

And wilt thou, coward-like, still spare the proud,
　　Who scorn thee in their hollow-hearted pride,
While still they'll toast thee, in a goblet, loud,
　　Around the crowded board, at eventide,

VI.

And strike the houseless wanderer on his road ?
　　And strip the cottage of its fragile roof ?
And crush its inmates as they kneel to God
　　Beneath the iron of thy conquering hoof ?

VII.

Its shivering inmates bid thee, pitying, stay ;
　　Its spoilless walls invite no robber bands ;
They feel the rugged force of Famine's sway,
　　And fear to meet thee with their fettered hands.

VIII.

There is not one who holds thy power in scorn,
   Or would not, in thy presence, freely bow ;
They pray to thee devoutly, night and morn,
   And do not curse thee when the fire burns low.

IX.

With broken swords, they have no hearts to fight,
   With stores, all wasted, courage quickly goes :
Men feel like children in the dead of night,
   And cry for help, and mercy from their foes.

WEEP NOT FOR ME.

—

I.

WEEP not for me—though our valleys be red
With the blood of the fallen—encumbered with dead ;
But weep for thy love, if thy love e'er returns,
While Freedom lies prostrate, and Erin still mourns.
Fair Liberty's host be no coward among,
No heart but the brave heart—no arm but the strong ;
And Friendship and Love be as nothing to me,
Till the land of my fathers be that of the free.

II.

Weep not for me—it is madness in love,
Till our country reclaims her proud treasure trove ;—
No sigh for the fallen—no tear for the slain,
Till that treasure by blood shall be purchased again.
Sorrow has loosened the minstrel's cord,
Tears have long rusted the patriot's sword ;
Bid the harp be restrung, and the sword flash again,
Till Liberty leaps from the souls of the slain !

UP, BROTHERS, UP.

Up, brothers, up!—the moon has departed,
   And you may be free ere the dawning of light;
Remember, your fathers were free and stout-hearted
   And rushed, like a torrent, to foray and fight.
You remember their war-cry, o'er hill and dale ringing,
   And the corse-covered field when the conflict was o'er,
And closer than all to your memories clinging,
   The freedom and fame of old Africa's shore.
Up, brothers, up! ere the red sun shall glisten,
   Up, brothers, up! ere the dawning of day;
Yon mountains are bending their huge heads to listen,
   And the ship's in the harbour, to bear you away.

II.

Shall the sons of her stalwart-limbed spearmen and bowmen,
   Ere a battle is ventured, account it as lost?
Shall the sons of brave sires make phantoms of foemen,
   And start, as a child starts, at goblin or ghost?

With the blood of such fathers, you cannot die craven ;
　　With a thought for their fame, you dare not so live ;
But brave as a lion and swift as the raven,
　　In the blood of your tyrants you'll find your reprieve.
Up, brothers, up ! ere the red sun shall glisten,
　　Up, brothers, up! ere the dawning of day ;
Yon mountains are bending their huge heads to listen,
　　And the ship's in the habour to bear you away.

ON SEEING A BUTTERFLY IN THE CITY.

I.

WHAT whimsical madness has led thee to roam
   From the green, sunny banks and the daisy-pied plain?
This is surely no spot for a butterfly's home,
   Where the rough-quarried stones hide the grass in the
      lane :
Where each field is a city, each garden a town,
   And the hamlets are crowded by women and men ;
Where the trees of the orchard, long rudely torn down,
   Will never be proud of their fruitage again.

II.

Have the soft, sunny winds of the south ceased to blow?
   The sun lost its way in a dull, misty sky?
Has the air ceased to ring with the musical flow
   Of the waters, whose channels were never a-dry?
Has the canker-worm eaten each blossom away?
   The locust consumed every morsel of green?
Or do mildew and blight hold tyrannical sway
   In the wide spreading valleys of nature's demesne?

III.

Oh, what could have tempted a butterfly here,
  From the green, grassy floor, and the clear azure sky?
Where only the captive bird's song greets the ear,
  And the plants in their infancy sicken and die?
Is it crime, or ambition, or folly, or hate,
  Or love of adventure, that leads thee astray?
Or hast thou been brought in a slumbrous state,
  Concealed in a garland of white-blossomed May?

IV.

If innocent yet, haste away to the grove:
  Let Distraction no more rob thy home of its peace;
Give the mate thou hast wronged a renewal of love,
  And let the career of the wanderer cease.
Return, thou frail beauty, ere night shall come on,
  Ere Danger shall threaten and hem thee around;
Return, now the brink of destruction is won—
  The wide, gaping portal of danger is found.

V.

Not a green leaf for shelter, no friend to console,
  A wilderness void of a branch or a stem.
Oh, if thou hast friends with thy fate to condole,
  Leave this land of Gomorrah and consort with them.

Like the poor, wingless moth who has danced round the
    flame,
For awhile, thou mayst wander the street without harm;
But the season will come when the red glare of shame
    Shall catch thy frail beauty and blight every charm.

TOIL ON, TOIL ON.

I.

Toil on, toil on, the golden age,
    The poet's scornéd fiction,
Has yet to come, and bear the cross
    Of Labour's crucifixion.
I care not for the nuggets found,
    The gold for which you've panted;
If happiness remains unfound,
    The rarest nugget's wanted !

II.

Though streams were changed to liquid gold,
    And pearls lay thick around us,
They need not make us wiser men,
    Nor happier than they found us:
Men sell their souls for love of gain,
    Till God by gold's supplanted;
Yet happiness remains unfound,
    The rarest nugget's wanted !

III.

A painted bubble floats to view,
  With eager eyes men watch it,
And vainly chase the empty prize,
  Exploded ere they catch it :
Delve, delve, and rock your cradled ore,
  Till honesty's recanted !
Fill, fill your coffers to the brim,
  And still the nugget's wanted !

ON SEEING HOOD'S GRAVE.

I.

THE spirit sleeps that erst with ardour wrought,
The mind is still that teemed with busy thought;
The thought-directed hand that grasped the plume,
Lies cold and stiffened in the silent tomb.
Weep, sisters, weep, for him who sang our woes,
And won us friendship from a world of foes!

PICTURES ON THE WALL.

I.

The poet's page may give delight,
  The sage's lore may teach;
But there are crushed and hidden hearts
  They vainly strive to reach.
Is there no way of moving these—
  Must they still lower fall?
We'll try the graver and the brush—
  The picture on the wall.

II.

The child intently gazes now,
  The eyes of age grow bright,
As they behold the wondrous power
  Of mingled shade and light.
From out those old, worm-eaten frames
  True angel-voices call,
And miracles are fairly wrought
  By pictures on the wall

D

III.

There are two teachers, ever young,
    The poet and the sage,
Who wage eternal war with Wrong,
    In every clime and age:
The world looks brighter through their leaves,
    In spring or summer's fall;
But you may see a world as bright
    In pictures on the wall.

———————

THE TRANSFIGURATION.

Oh! Heaven! it was a fearful wind, so wondrous large with
    hatred,
It seemed to covet for its wrath all God and man hold
    sacred:
It struck a ship whose idle sails against its sides were
    flapping,
And tore its planks asunder all, till ribs like mouths were
    gaping.
It smote huge trees, and rocks, and hills; it howled like
    blatant thunder,
It crossed a temple on its way and tore its aisles asunder.

Hid from its wrath, I sat and watched a sorely wounded
    plover
Sink down in secrecy to die among the three-leaved clover;
But oh! it was too soon to die in summer time so early,
And leave its little brood to pine among the bearded barley.

"Thrice welcome Death," the bird exclaimed, as though it
     brought a treasure,
" I've sipped too long the bitterness of life's deceitful
     measure ;
I'll hide me here and give my breath to gain a new dominion,
Where I can soar for evermore on new and tireless pinion.
Roar on, wild wind, my requiem sing, I will not meet
     Death trembling,
The wound thou gav'st is mortal, past healing, past dis-
     sembling."

Oh, God! how hellish false my tale—'twas not a wounded
     plover
That sank in secrecy to die, among the three-leaved clover ;
No, no! 'twas woman, woe-enslaved, with temples hot and
     aching,
That cried for death, a speedy death, to ease her heart from
     breaking ;
Not fledglings of a wounded bird excited my poor pity,
But, God, it was the motherless, left weeping in the city !
The bearded barley but the wealth by bristling bayonets
     guarded,
Aye flaunted in the sight of those whom Fortune hath
     discarded.

'Twas not the savage onslaughts of the wind that wakes the
　　ocean
That drove her back, and slew her, ere she reached her little
　　Goshen;
But wilder storms of reinless strife, of seething, unquenched
　　rancour,
That breed despair in women's souls, and tear them from
　　their anchor.
The temple that was rent in twain was not the dwarfed and
　　simple,
But richer far—the human soul's own great and wondrou
　　temple,
That, daily shattered, lets poor souls into the world go
　　wandering,
While men, like gamesters, little deem the riches they are
　　squandering:
And, oh! that doomed, devoted ship, that was so richly
　　laden,
Hast thou not seen a rudderless, a weak, half-crazéd maiden
That once was seen to sit and rule the waves on which she
　　sported,
Borne by the wind and rent and torn, and fearfully deserted?
The rocks, the pines, and hills hard struck, were truths built
　　up by ages,

But these were safe, and Hell's fierce wrath against them idly
    rages ;
All truths from Heaven are guarded from the time they reach
    Earth's portal,
And walk the earth like angels, unclothéd and immortal.
Oh ! Hell of Earth ! Oh ! Paradise ! Oh ! shunned ! Oh !
    sought and treasured,
How falsely are thy bitters and thy sweets to mortals
    measured !
How some will cling to this poor earth as though their lives
    were bounded
By those receding walls of sky by which they are surrounded.
Some wildly and despairingly will cut their lives asunder,
And make the worldly drop their scales and hold their
    breath in wonder ;
But little mends the wonderment of those who think so
    rarely,
The cry of woe escapes their ear amidst the bearded barley !

BEN THE MINER.

I.

In the grave of the forest, grim-featured, we found him,
    Brave, sturdy Ben;
Where his deeds for the love of humanity crowned him
    A king among men.

II.

Strong of limb, though the fire of his youth had departed—
    A glance from his eye,
Proved his claim to be ranked with the true and stout-hearted
    Who fear not to die.

III.

When Confusion and Death (oft the children of Error)
    Were raging around,
With the soul of a warrior, proof against terror,
    He'd ever been found.

IV.

From the deep sulph'rous pit, where the fiery blast, howling,
    Daringly bold,
He had oft rescued life, while grim Death yet lay scowling
    Down tho grim hold.

V.

Still he knew not the fame the world had accorded
    For courage so true,
And he knew not the wealth which even the sordid
    Had voted his due.

VI.

When we mentioned his fame, ho would scarcely believe it
    Was fairly his own;
When we offered him wealth he was loth to receive it,
    Though valiantly won.

SAMSON.

" When he raiseth up himself, the mighty are afraid."

I.

Strong Samson's sleeping, soundly sleeping,
  With false Delilah's arms around him ;
The Philistines are slily creeping,
  That once with ropes and withes had bound him.
Encircled in her snowy arms,
  He thought not—dreamt not—of her guile,—
She won his secret with her charms,
  And slew a giant with a smile !

II.

" Let every Philistine assemble,
  And share the triumph of our race ;
See Israel's chosen warrior tremble,
  Behold their 'God of gods'' disgrace !
To Dagon let all praise be given—
  Proclaim his victory far and near ;

We scorn their God, and doubt their heaven—
   And all his boasted vengeance dare!
Where is the Jew who slew our brothers—
   Who burst our gates, and burnt our corn?
Bring—bring him forth—let wives and mothers—
   Thirsting for vengeance—hurl their scorn!
Let every Philistine that feared him
   Glorify 'God' at his disgrace;
Let every child that trembled, beard him!
   Till tears roll down his eyeless face!"

III.

From Gath and Ekron crowds assemble,
   From Beer and Timna myriads come,
To see their ancient foeman tremble
   Within their sea-god's—Dagon's—home!
The rich, the poor, the wise, the simple,
   The young, the old, in love and fear,
Laden with gifts for Dagon's temple,
   Fruit of labour, spoil of war.

IV.

A human sea fills every space,
   The roof, the temple, and its court;

And, eager for their foe's disgrace,
 They seek the soul-beguiling sport.
Child-led, in prayer-like attitude,
 God's warrior stands amid the crowd ;
And list'ning to their jestings rude,
 He breathes this heart-felt prayer aloud :—

V.

"Revenge! revenge! oh, Israel's God!
 Revenge the piercing of these eyes !—
They tear me from my vile abode
 To mock my keenest agonies!
Look on thy servant, pale, and weak,
 And penitent—besmeared with blood!
Give back my giant-strength to wreak
 Eternal hate on this vile brood !"

VI.

Behold ! the pillars fly asunder!
 An awful shriek—and one short breath—
A sudden crash like Heaven's thunder,
 And Dagon's triumph ends in death!

VII.

Where their scoffing ?—where their laughter ?
  Where their mirth, and where their cheering ?
Where their god in beam or rafter ?
  Where their mockery ?—where their jeering?
Where the payment for the treasures
  Sacrificed at Dagon's throne ?
Where the wisdom of their measures?
  Where their earth-born powers gone ?
Lost for ever! and their pride,
  Lust for greed and gain they cherished —
Gone!   The cheat they deified !
  Temple, throne, and shrine, have perished !

VIII.

Lab'rers ! lab'rers ! are ye sleeping !
  Know ye not this giant strong !
Know ye not his kindred weeping
  'Neath fraud, contumely and wrong !
Know ye not each spoil receiver —
  Fattening, while ye starve and die !
Giving gold to the deceiver—
  Whose existence is a lie !

By their lust of greed ye know them—
  By their every act and crime !
Ye have strength to overthrow them,
  Labour, Samson of all time !

TWAS DOWN IN A VALLEY.

I.

'Twas down in a valley, where wild flowers grew,
    I met my dear Jenny one day;
She blamed me for flirting with Katty and Sue,
    And bade me begone, lack-a-day!
The frown on her face was killed by a smile,
    Yet, unheeding, I turned to depart;
But, before I could place my right foot on the stile,
    She cried—"I forgive you, sweetheart:
    Come back, I forgive you, sweetheart."

II.

The wounded in love are not swift o'th' wing,
    Injured pride seldom quickens delay;
E'en pigeons, though woundless, will fly in a ring
    And consider—thought I, lack-a-day!
Thus I said, while I balanced the frown with a smile,
    "Is it better to stay or to part?"
Then I turned like a truant away from the stile,
    And cried, "I forgive you, sweetheart,
    As thou hast forgiven, sweetheart."

SONNET.

I.

Oh ! honoured tree to shade so rich a tomb!
A nation's tears shall yet increase thy growth,
And gift thee with an everlasting youth !
And many children to thy shrine will come,
From loom, and plough, and mine, and troubled home ;
From lands afar—east, north, and west, and south—
Brave seekers of a pure and stainless truth,
Whose triumph lies in Time's prolific womb.
In days unborn, a freedom loving throng
Shall here assemble, and tho shout, " Wo're free !"
Re-echo mid tho tombs ; and Fraud and Wrong
Have less of life than frail Mortality ;
And o'en thy drooping boughs shall gaze on heaven,
So much of lusty life by Freedom shall be given.

THE DREAM OF THE MILLENNIUM.

I DREAMT a dream of happiness—it fell
  Upon me softly as an Eastern rain!
The earth was changed for lands where angels dwell.
  Old Eden's grandeur clothed the world again.
The fertile plain, the fen, and marsh, and moor,
  Had cast away their sterile garb of old,
When Fiction wrote the feastings of the poor,
  And tyrants ruled, and fettered slaves rebelled.
The wailing curlew sang a bridal song,
  The mourning cypress wore a gayer hue,
The sered heart suddenly grew green and strong,
  And all men loved the beautiful and true!
The priests were changed for poets—poets, those
  Who gave contentment to the troubled soul,
And pluck'd the sting from death—soothed labour throes,
  Bade man be free, and made the wounded whole;
Spoke with impassioned tongues of living truth,
  Acted their Godlike creeds before men's eyes;

Gave to the worn-out world a deathless youth,
   As pure as snow in earth's first paradise.
Or fringed the darkest clouds of heaven with smiles,
   Or painted roses on the palest cheek—
With daring hands unbound Sin's serpent coils,
   And spoke to common men as angels speak.
I felt as though my nature had been changed,
   As though all evil had been torn away ;
All thoughts of guile were from my heart estranged,
   And Justice gloried in unfettered sway.
I woke ! an ebon darkness filled the air,
   Nor moon, nor star, hung in the vaulted heaven ;
I knelt me down, and bowed my soul in prayer,
   And vigil kept till morn had darkness riven ;
When sullenly the darkness broke away,
   And streams of light climbed up the eastern sky ;
My soul looked out upon Earth's new-born day,
   And Sin was there, and Want, and Misery.
" O God !" I cried, "and is it but a dream ?"
   " No more, vain man—long vigil thou must keep—
Life's dark path lighted by a fitful gleam,
   That steals across your vision when asleep."

ENCOURAGEMENT.

I.

On, do not grieve, my own dear wife,
  The cloud will pass away ;
There's health and vigour in the strife
  That brings your soul to bay :
I would not, had I strength, control
  The furies of the sky,
While there are powers within the soul,
  That storms can only try.

II.

Have faith in Him who reigns above,
  He guards both me and you ;
By strife alone He tests our love,
  And proves it false or true.
I would not ride on land-locked seas,
  Untried by storm or gale :
I glory in the stirring breeze
  That threatens every sail.

III.

I would not fly from hope and life,
   Or, coward-like, despair
When Courage whispers, "Brave the strife,
   And happiness is near;"
Nor would I, like a swallow, fly
   The land that gave me birth,
Because a cloud bedimmed the sky,
   Or thunder shook the earth.

EARTHLY PERFECTION.

It is not an idle fancy that the best are called away,

While the wicked and the worthless make on earth the
longest stay ;

None can leave us who are sinful; they must stay and be
forgiven :

Those who leave the world behind them have been rendered
fit for heaven.

In the graveyard by the seashore I have sat and watched
the waves

Disinterring men and women from their ill-protected
graves ;

They were there to rot and fester, some were changing into
clay ;

I could see naught like perfection—it alone had passed
away.

I have marked the meek-eyed violet in the deep, sequestered
dell,

And the pure and spotless lily by the silver-footed rill,

Till naught was left but faded leaves and petals sickly pale,

That crept into earth's bosom at the bidding of the gale.

I have often heard the sweet-tongued lark appeal to heaven
      in vain,

As the clouds drew wide asunder to admit the heavenly
      strain ;

But ere it reached heaven's portal, all perfection rose to God,

And the bird came wandering back once more to man's
      unclean abode.

Through the broadway of the evening, I have stood and
      watched afar,

The headlong passage of the lost and heaven-discarded star ;

I have watched it coming earthward from the high and
      glittering dome,

To mingle with the fallen in man's purgatorial home.

I have listened to the streamlet, as it sang without a care,

And watched an essence rising from its bosom like a prayer ;

I have seen it rising upward till the clouds began to lower,

But the stain of earth was on it, and it came down with the
      shower.

I have marked the feathered arrow, as it clove the open sky

With its wild and fierce ambition to penetrate on high,

And I have marked its headlong course, as back to earth it
      came,

And plunged itself deep in the earth to hide its burning
    shame.

All the dross of heaven falls earthward, and the dust of
    angels' feet

Falls on us and around us, and admits of no retreat;

Still God is with us here on earth, He makes the wild birds
    sing,

And bids the sweet-mouthed flowers heed the summons of
    the spring.

He rules the mighty ocean, rides unseen upon the breeze,

And abideth in the caverns of the deep, unfathomed seas;

And each may mark His footprints and follow where He trod,

As each may feel the presence of the Omnipresent God.

But none can touch perfection; it is His and His alone,

And it leaveth all the planets to concentrate in one!

Who art thou, thou mighty preacher, with thy tongue to
    charm all ears,

Calling God to test the virtue of thy penitential tears?

Who art thou, crowned king of nations, calling heaven to
    mark thy sway

Over slaves who've learned the lesson to be humble and
    obey?

Art thou perfect in thy dealings,—justly using sword and
    pen?

Then the earth has found an angel to subdue the souls of
    men!
Clouds shall vanish, error quit us, and the falling dews and
    rain,
Shall redeem the land we tread on from the curse of taint
    and stain
And perfection shall be with us; it shall rest like moun-
    tain snow
On the hilltops in its passage to the sinful world below;
It shall spread, like snow dissolving, through the plains and
    vales beneath,
And impregnate every atom with an everlasting breath;
Till the earth is earth no longer, and till men are men no
    more,
But a band of sinless angels linked to heaven for evermore.

A GLORIOUS TRIO.

————

I.

To brigands and robbers I care not to toast,
    While piratical knaves I abhor ;
But bold Robin Hood of the merry green wood
    Fought the battle of England's poor ;
'Twas not plunder that led him to foray and fight,
    Nor to dwell in the merry green wood :
But a burning desire to stand by the right,
    And contest with the foeman each rood.
        So fill up your can—drink, drink, every man,
            In remembrance of brave Robin Hood.

II.

I've another toast yet, so be wary, my boys,
    Of the depths of each can that ye take ;
I've a hero as good as the brave Robin Hood—
    Here's the almost forgotten Le Wake.

When the coward knelt down to the Norman in fear,
 He crouched in the deep-bosomed glen,
Yet, not like the coward, devoid of his spear,
 But armed to the teeth like his men.
  So drink the can dry to his brave memory,
   Here's Hereward, Lord of the Fen.

III.

Hold, hold, my brave boys, I've another toast left,
 Do not drink as though toasting was o'er;
I've a hero whose name shall be rescued from shame
 By the freemen who people our shore;
Here's Tyler, brave Tyler, of poll tax renown,
 Who slew the King's minion one day,
Then marched with his friends up to famed London town,
 And kept the King's army at bay.
  Drink, drink to the dregs, till you're weak in
   the legs,
   For a glorious trio were they.

THE SOUNDS OF LABOUR.

I.

I LOVE the sound of the woodman's axe
   As it falls on the sturdy oak ;
And the sound of the flail on the threshing floor,
   Ere the morn has fairly broke ;
The cheerful smack of the teamster's whip,
   By the heavily-laden wain ;
And the mingled sounds from the harvest field,
   As I pass down the old green lane.
For they tell how thought and toil combined
   Can aid Creation's plan,
And multiply the wondrous gifts
   The soil bestows on man.

II.

I love the clack of the merry mill-wheel,
   The sound of the hammer's fall :
The ring of the shivering trowel, struck
   By the hand that rears the wall :

The dull dead sound of the pavior's blow,
  The rush of the passing train,
And the sailor's cry of " Yo, heave, ho!"
  Coming over the surging main.
For they tell how thought and toil combined,
  Can aid Creation's plan,
And multiply the wondrous gifts,
  The soil bestows on man.

III.

I love the sturdy collier's cry,
  The roar of the furnace strong:
The click of type on the printer's stick,
  And the shouts of the toiling throng:
The sound of the perilous grinder's stone,
  The jack of the knitter's frame,
The spinning lathe, and the smelter's blast,
  With its bursting sheet of flame.
For they tell how thought and toil combined
  Can aid Creation's plan,
And multiply the wondrous gifts
  The soil bestows on man.

THE BROTHERS.

WILLIAM.

I TELL thee thou art wrong to leave the world:
Its bustle is its life—ay, thine and mine:
And more, I hate the stupid pedantry
That seems to cling around thy studious ways.
There is a pride—a false, obtrusive pride—
That ever sits upon thy pensive brow;
It mocks mankind and cries, " Go, go thy way!
I'm not of thee, thou fleshpot of the world!"

HENRY.

Why blame your brother for the life he leads,
As though Seclusion wore the face of Crime?
When all was dark, ay, darker than the night,
The student's ill-fed lamp re-lit the world.

WILLIAM.

I've seen thine dimly burn night after night,
And I confess I've seen no magic power,

By which, if sun, and moon, and stars went out,
The world would be oblivious to their loss.

HENRY.

'Tis true.   I'm no magician, and my lamp
Was never trimmed by aught save human hands—
And yet the lamp that young Aladdin found
Was like to that, or all is fabled lies.

WILLIAM.

Go to thy lamp, and leave the world to me.

HENRY.

The student does not sicken of the world;
'Tis love that bids him leave it for awhile :
He then enrapt in gloomy solitude,
(Like he who stands in some dark entrance hid)
Sees more by far that's passing in the light
Than he who moves within its very blaze.
By light we see, and he who sees not light,
Sees not ; but by excess of light the eye
Is blinded.   All light is heat, and burns away
The sense of seeing as it fills the sight.

WILLIAM.

Go ; leave the world—it is not fit for thee,
And in thy dreams see heavens and call them down,

HENRY.

Is it a sin to dream and make earth heaven,
To see the white-winged angels hover round ?
Granting such heavens are but a sleeper's thoughts,
The fickle fancies of a spell-bound mind—
Still, where's the man who has not chased a shade
And found enjoyment nearer as he ran ?
Oh, speak no more, thou never canst speak true !
The thoughtful man is never left alone,
And they are wrong who deem him a recluse
Who has the power to people solitudes.
Good night ! good night !

WILLIAM.

Good night ! thou more than sun !

HONEST ROBIN'S SONG.

I.

ANOTHER stranger in the cot—the gracious gift of God,
A heaven-directed visitant to cheer our dull abode:
Another prop for mine old age, when winter's storms shall
      gather,
Still one more silver tongue to lisp the honoured name of
      father ;

II.

You sometime wail the lot, Mary, that we must fain endure,
But while we claim our children's love, we never can be
      poor !
I'd sooner see yon infant smile, and hear those cherubs sing,
Than sit upon an heirless throne, and be a childless king.

III.

Though our food be rude and scant, Mary, and proud men
      pass us by,
Can that bring sorrow to our hearts, and tears to your bright
      eye?
No, let them boast the untold wealth the untired sun goes
      round,
And we'll still shake hands with Poverty, where children's
      smiles abound.

IV.

We've lips that equal rubies, with living lustre shining,
We've golden-tinted ringlets, on necks of snow reclining;
We've teeth of pearl-like whiteness, we've eyes of sapphire
      hue,
And, better far, we've strong, sound hearts that never were
      untrue;

V.

We've wealth and independence in this strong right arm of
      mine,
You've still the trace of beauty in that honest face of thine;
And when the bleak winds whistle through the snow-charged
      realms above
You've a robin by your side, Mary, who'll sing you songs of
      love.

IDLE WORDS.

I.

How often is a loose, cross word
   The cause of endless woe and strife ?
A single angry passion stirred,
   Will oft embitter half a life :
A little thought, a moment's calm,
   When hearts are sorely rent in twain,
Will oft supply the healing balm,
   And join the severed cords again.

II.

The heat of youth is hard to cool,
   Beneath the rein 'twill chafe and fret;
But who will spurn fair Reason's rule
   To live a life of stern regret !
I would not quench life's glowing flame
   Before the spring of life is o'er ;
But, oh, I would, for very shame,
   Encompass it by all that's pure.

F.

III.

I warn the man, who, growing old,
   Is still a slave at Passion's feet;
But fain would shun the heart grown cold,
   Despoiled of Love's ennobling heat:
A steady flame, nor strong nor weak,
   Should ever burn at youth's fair prow;
A genial warmth is all I seek
   To keep the frost from Age's brow.

THE MOTHER AND CHILD.

I.

" Let us talk of the stars," said a flaxen haired girl,
  " Of the sun, and the moon, and the sea,
Of the gems of the ocean, the coral and pearl,
  And the flowers that bloom on the lea.
Do the stars bloom like daisies and wither away ?
  Do they slumber from morning till noon ?
And where do they hide themselves all the long day ?
  And is there a man in the moon ?
And tell me if mortal e'er ventured so far
On such wild giddy heights as yon brave little star ?

II.

" Let us talk of the sea—of its corals and pearls,
  Of its riches, its wonders, and worth,
  Of its sweet, pleasing face when it dances and whirls,
  And gives such soft mutterings birth,

Of its angry look when it foams and it raves,
    Or gloats o'er the wreck it has made;
And tell me when mariners go to their graves,
    Are no funeral prayers over said?
And tell me, dear mother, are pearls made from tears ?
And what formed the coral that baby now wears ?"

III.

" The stars, my dear child, do not wither away,
    Nor slumber from morning till noon ;
They watch through the night till the dawning of day,"—
    " Till summoned away by the moon ?"
" Ah, no, my dear child, 'tis the earth that moves round,
    To be warmed by the light of the sun;
The stars, keeping watch, in the heavens may be found,
    In nations where night has begun ;
They have no time for leisure, for frolic or fun,
Their watch is unceasing—their work never done.

IV

" There are islands, my child, in the midst of the sea,
    That seem to be fashioned from stone ;
But those who look keenly, in wonderment, see,
    They are formed by the coral alone:

But of pearls, my dear child, ah, what can I tell?
　　They are found by brave venturesome men
In the home of the fish—on its hard rocky shell,
　　And they say they are tears born of pain.
Those bearers of incense, the flowers, my child,
Burst laughingly forth when Eden first smiled.

v.

"The passionate sea is a child in God's hand,
　　Grasped firmly by him evermore,
He bids it to crumble the rock into sand,
　　Or sport like a child on the shore:
Each mortal will join th' awakening host,
　　No matter where resteth his load,
And he that goes down with the ship that is lost,
　　Is never forgotten by God.
The souls of the righteous climb upward afar,
And look down on the earth like yon brave little star.

VI.

"Creation, my child, is the great work of God,
　　And includes everything that we see,
From the tiniest flower that springs from the sod
　　To Nature's great wonder—the sea!

Those magical caves with their festoons of spars,
 Whose beauties bedazzle thine eye ;
The great dome of heaven—its sun, moon, and stars—
 The life of earth, ocean and sky!
The hues of the rainbow, the scent of earth's flowers,
The slow rising mist, and the fast-falling showers."

A BALLAD.

I.

THE fire of youth few years will quench,
  But there's still warmth enough within,
And I have felt, my bonny wench,
  That Youth may lose and Age may win :
The day must wane, the night will come,
  And summer's heat bring winter's cold,
But nought but joy shall fill our home
  Though we be getting old, Dame.

II.

Thank God we've led a godly life,
  And dare look back and scan our way ;
We know no hours of burning strife
  To haunt us now we're growing grey.

Our daughters heed the lessons taught,
  Our sons have never caused a tear,
And long and honestly they've wrought
  Thine heart and mine to cheer, Dame.

III.

Thy spinning wheel has long been still,
  My palsied hand has rested long,
But yet we share our frugal meal
  As though we were still hale and strong;
My heart is full of varied joys
  That kings would give a world to see,
When I behold our girls and boys
  So good to you and me, Dame.

ON THE SEA-SHORE.

SHADOW.

I.

As I stood and watched the ocean
 Throw its warm waves on the shore,
Like a pulse, each tidal effort,
 Throbbing, throbbing, evermore ;
Winds were calm and gave no motion,
 But the fretful fall and swell
Of the sea bespoke its anguish
 Better far than tongue can tell:

II.

" I am rolling over riches,
 I have parted land from land,
I have buried untold cities
 With my gold and silver sand ;

I have wrung men's souls with sorrow,
   Shook the manliest heart with fears,
While I grow in strength and grandeur
   From the mighty tide of tears.

III.

"Tears of mothers, tears of children,—
   Widows, orphans, I have made;
Tears of cheated bride and bridegroom,
   In their bridal clothes arrayed:
Tears of men from wives long parted,
   Tears that leave their trace behind,
In the cheek and brow's deep furrows,
   And the scorchings of the mind."

IV.

Sad at heart I wandered homeward,
   Through each field of ripening corn,
With its golden tinge of autumn
   That entrancéd me at morn;
All earth's grandeur had departed,
   Shadows spread o'er tower and tree,
I could only hear the moaning
   Of the sad and troubled sea.

SUNSHINE.

V.

On the morrow, by the sea-shore,
   Sad and silently I strayed,
Till I heard a loud voice ringing,
   " Up! and get your anchor weigh'd !
Spread your canvas to the wind, boys,
   Let our brave ship tempt the seas ;
There's rare promise in the morning,
   Not a whistle in the breeze."

VI.

Willing hearts obey the summons,
   Sturdy seamen crowd the deck :
Men who will not shrink from duty,
   Though it bound them to a wreck.
Up aloft the wide sails spreading,
   Round and round the windlass flew ;
Will the rudder steer the vessel
   As the captain guides the crew ?

VII.

There is merchandise within her,
   British mail-bags crowd her hold,

And many a burning passion
  Could the freighted ship unfold !
She's afloat upon the waters,
  Like a thing to life allied,
And, rejoicing in her freedom,
  Fairly dances on the tide.

VIII.

The sun shines bright before her,
  She is favoured by the wind,
While affection from the waters
  Casts a silver streak behind ;
And a sudden joy comes o'er me
  As I watch her quit the strand,
Fairly healing up the chasm
  That has parted land from land.

IX.

She will join long-severed kindred,
  Bid the prodigal return,
Stir the embers of affection
  That, in absence, ceased to burn ;

Dry the tears of weeping mothers,
   Give to fathers sudden joys,
By recounting all the honours
   That have fallen on their boys.

X.

She will speak the latest gospel,
   She will tell the newest truth,
She will give the lore of nations
   Unto nations in their youth ;
She will bind men's souls together
   By the knowledge of the free ;
She is walking o'er the waters
   As the Saviour trod the sea.

XI.

Joyously the rock ascending
   By a strangely fretted path,
With its balusters of scroll-work
   That bespoke the sad sea's wrath,
Quick ! the precious truth thrilled through me,
   There's no sorrow in the wave,
But the sea retains the saltness
   That its mother, Nature, gave !

XII.

It protects it in its calmness,
  While it guards it in the strife;
Who would dare to change its flavour,
  When its flavour is its life?
Then, again returning homeward,
  Through each field of ripening corn,
I beheld earth's glowing grandeur
  That entrancéd me at morn.

SAINTED WINIFRED.

I.

'Thou hadst once a sister fair,
Blue eyes and golden hair—
But Death came here one day,
And led the child away!
'Twas in the winter's gloom
Our house became a tomb,
Death heeding not our prayer,
Blue eyes, nor golden hair!

II.

Behold the fairest flower
That drank of dew or shower,
Hath perished of decay
Erewhile it reached its May ;
Behold its slender wand
Lies parchéd on the strand,
Its petals, rainbow-hued,
Around the wand bestrewed.

III.

But flowers thus early perished,
By angel hands are cherished ;
They bloom on Heaven's greensward,
By the footsteps of the Lord,
And in that blessed retreat,
Are trod by angel-feet,
Till gathered for their graces
And pressed to angel-faces.

THE WEAVER'S SONG.

I.

The spring-time of life has departed,
  And summer, blythe summer, has come,
To find me, alas, broken-hearted,
  And chained like a slave to the loom.
The fairy-like patterns I'm weaving
  Are like the bright fancies I wove,
Ere my spirit was broken by grieving,
  And Fate told the folly of love.

II.

In the heaven-born design I am working,
  I see nought of sorrow or gloom,
And yet there's a thought ever lurking
  That prisons my soul to the loom ;
And thus, from the dawn of the morning,
  The real drives the ideal away ;
Till Night, with its shadows returning,
  Shrouds every hope in dismay.

III.

Kind heaven, give me strength but to plan some
   Escape from the torments I feel;
But death holds the only ransom,
   And dying's the only ordeal.
How soft is the velvet I'm weaving,
   How hard is the fate I've to bear!
And yet what a folly is grieving,
   When grief leads to woe and despair.

WE HAVE NOTHING TO FEAR.

I.

We have nothing to fear, when a tinker in jail (1)
  Can audience claim from a king,
And a cobbler (2) in prison finds nought to bewail,
  So contentedly sits down to sing;
When a ploughman, (3) a beggar, (4) a poor peasant youth, (5)
  A shepherd (6) while tending his fold,
Enrich their rare songs with the flavour of truth,
  And shame the rich minstrels of old!
      We've nothing to fear,
      We've plenty to cheer,
        The future is ours, hurrah!

II.

We have nothing to fear, when a poor trapper lad, (7)
  Gives to mankind the wings of a bird,

---

(1) John Bunyan (2) Thomas Cooper, author of "Purgatory of Suicides." (3) Burns. (4) Willie Thom. (5) John Clare. (6) Hogg, the Ettrick Shepherd. (7) Robert Stephenson.

When Science comes forth in her working robes clad,
  And the sweet voice of Wisdom is heard :
When a barber (1) sits down by his own fire-side,
  In the midst of his children at play,
And resolves, in despite of his garrulous bride,
  How the world can be clothed in a day.
              We've nothing to fear,
              We've plenty to cheer,
                The future is ours, hurrah !

III.

We have nothing to fear, for Justice shall reign,
  And distinguish the right from the wrong :
And the glory of craft, like a meteor, shall wane,
  In the midday of science and song :
When the full voice of Freedom shall clearly be heard,
  Waking echoes from mountain and glen,
And the innermost depths of men's souls shall be stirred,
  And the truth rise triumphant again.
              We've nothing to fear,
              We've plenty to cheer,
                The future is ours, hurrah !

        (1) Arkwright.

BESSIE.

Our hearts were so tender, our years were so few,
   And yet we enjoyed the most exquisite bliss,
As we sat 'neath the shade of the wide-spreading yew,
And watched the cloud-vessels skim under the blue.

The soft-noted linnet sang songs by our side,
   As though he had shared in the rapture we felt ;
The silvery troutlet sprang high o'er the tide,
And stole a sly glance at my beautiful bride.

Each daisy a-tiptoe looked over the green,
   To see beauty rarer than daisy can boast,
And all the gay creatures that filled up the scene
Were beauties attendant on Beauty's own queen.

If you e'er saw a flower, 'tween budding and bloom,
   When your lips are in doubt if breathing its name,
If you e'er saw the sun just escaping from gloom,
Or the first blush of morning when Summer has come,

You have seen naught so fair, though all did combine,
  No pencil could paint her, no chisel pourtray ;
Her beauties, aye changing, yet ever divine,
Even Jove had preferred to Juno and wine.

II.

By the Colne-side, spirit-laden,
  I have wandered long ago,
With a sweet and dainty maiden,
  Sacred source of all my woe ;
Purest, fairest, of Eve's daughters,
  She had pledged her heart to me ;
But the babbling, smooth-tongued waters
  Told her beauty to the sea.

And the story so beguiling
  To Old Ocean's mind did prove,
That he told the same tale smiling
  To the earth, his lady-love ;
When one, Death, he heard the story
  Of my fairy-featured bride,
And he stole Earth's crowning glory
  When he snatched her from my side.

III.

The words spent their force on the warm thoughts that
  filled me,
 When they told me my Bessie was gone to her grave ;
And Disbelief saved, when belief would have killed me,
 As dangers unfelt leave the timid heart brave.

The words fell as waves fell, all scattered around me,
 Their unity broken to gather again,
When bereft of those warm thoughts returning they found
  me,
 To crush me with anguish and rack me with pain.
Sad at heart, by the Colne-side, I silently wandered,
 And its musical ripple was music no more ;
And many a lone sigh in anguish I squandered,
 For many vain hopes I had cherished before.

I stood at the spot where the stream is divided,
 And each takes its weary way down to the sea,
Lamenting the loss of a grandeur so prided,
 And dear to its glory as Bessie to me.

Each passed on its way, and I left them for ever,
 To wander heart-broken, with Grief for a bride,
And no more shall an angel-face peer from the river,
 Since Death slew the angel that walked by its side.

IV.

"She has gone;" they whispered softly,
    "Her fair spirit's taken flight;"
And my heart was crushed within me,
    Day departed ere 'twas night;
Then the gay earth lost its gladness,
    Bursting blossoms died in June,
And a cloud seemed ever hanging
    In the face of star and moon.

And the birds that sang so sweetly
    In the meadow and the grove,
Sang a strange and mournful ditty,
    As though each had lost its love;
And the scenes where we had wandered,
    Grew more hateful day by day,
As though Death had disrobed Nature,
    When he stole my love away.

V.

Rude were the songs that I framed for my Bessie;
    Yet doubtless to her they had many a spell;
Rudely I sang them, but never dreamed Bessie,
    That any but angels could sing them so well;

She told me the Bird o' the Morn was outrivalled,
　Outrivalled the songsters that wakened the grove;
That her ears were aye closed to their wordless out-pourings,
　Since I fashioned her songs from the lava of love.

But I know not, alas, what sad change has come o'er me,
　For my life is a long and continuous dream,
Where all is removed that was wont to inspire me,
　For Heaven claimed the beauty that furnished my
　　theme:
Fair Nature is charmless—I fly to her bowers;
　Yet Grief tracks my footsteps wherever I go;
The shade of my Bessie has left them for ever,
　And Earth is to me but a picture of woe.

VI.

The Spring has lost its freshness,
　The Summer beauty's gone,
The autumn is less golden,
　The Winter cold and lone;
The morning ever dim, now,
　Disrobed of all its light;
And empty as a shell, floats
　The gorgeous lamp o' night;

I used to love the meadows
   Where the flowers bloom and die ;
But now my flowers are stars, love,
   That blossom in the sky ;
I used to love the linnet
   For his music-making throat :
But now I watch the lark, love,
   Through boundless ether float.

I thought this dull earth heaven, love,
   When thou wert here below ;
'Tis now a realm of darkness,
   Brimful of burning woe ;
Brimful of burning woe, love,
   I cast my eyes above ;
And every planet shining
   Seems a fitting home for love.

I saw Death at your side, love,
   With aspect fierce and wild ;
He takes me by the hand, love,
   And leads me like a child ;

He takes me by the hand, love,
   And no convulsive start,
Disturbs this shattered frame, love,
   Or chills this lonely heart ;
With fingers raised to Heaven, love,
   He bids me think of thee,
And leaves my soul a prisoned bird
   That panteth to be free.

GATHER YE, GATHER YE.

I.

The rain would be wasted that falls on the mountains,
  Did Labour not delve in the valleys below ;
Kind heaven would be thrifty and dry up her fountains
  If Labour withdrew its strong arm from the plough.
Gather ye, gather ye, boldest and bravest,
  Rush to the valley and rush to the plain ;
"And the earth that ye tickle shall laugh through the
      harvest,"
And quaff ye in bumpers of fast-flowing rain.

II.

When the broad-footed oxen trod Egypt's rich valleys,
  And Labour inscribed on each acre a prayer ;
Joy reigned in her courts, and mirth in her alleys,
  And rustling cornflags waved high in the air.
But now ye may tread o'er the land that lies burning,
  But tread o'er it lightly, 'tis proud Egypt's grave,
And behold 'mid her ruins the trace of her learning,
  And sigh for lost treasures that burdened the wave.

III.

Gather ye, gather ye, boldest and bravest,
    Gather in earnest to labour and moil,
Till the voice of the Lord shall awaken the harvest
    That fell fast asleep on Egypt's rich soil.
Its ears have been pricked by the Lord's roaring thunder,
    Watch ye its rising as one who has slept;
Count ye it's green flags that wave beyond number,
    Behold the lost glory that nations have wept.

NO MORE I'LL SIGH FOR VANISHED JOYS.

I.

No more I'll sigh for vanished joys,
   Nor o'er them vainly ponder ;
There is no worth in broken toys,
   Nor old loves torn asunder.
Are there no joys which never fade,
   That we may fondly treasure ?
Nor vainly cleave to things decayed,
   And hug the empty measure !

II.

A flower crushed will fade away
   And breathe forth all its sweetness;
But plant its seed deep in the clay,
   And it will reach completeness.
While thus our joys ne'er bloom again,
   Still cleaving to the bosom,
Are seeds of vanquished joy and pain
   That smiles or tears will blossom.

THE GOLDEN TEMPTER.

I.

ONE had wealth, another beauty ;
　　Oh, 'twas hard indeed to choose ;
Either prize was worth the winning,
　　Each too great by far to lose ;
One was rich, and one was handsome,
　　Wealth was ugly, Beauty poor ;
Beauty maketh Wealth more wealthy,
　　Wealth increases Beauty's store.

II.

" Rob the one, and wed the other ;"
　　Silence, tempter, get thee gone ;
What are both, devoid of honour ?
　　Worse than either when alone.
Conscience is not bribed by riches,
　　Wealth is not a salve for crime ;
Crime will stain the soul for ever,
　　Conscience rack you in your prime.

III.

Limbs to labour, brain to guide them,
 Health to keep them firm and strong;
And a lass, brimful of beauty,
 Are a fortune to the young.
These are mine, and shall I leave them,
 Cozened by deceitful gold;
Get thee gone, thou bold deceiver,—
 Tempt me when I'm getting old.

HERNE'S OAK.

Oft I think of the time when a sapling I stood,
And the lands, now unclothed, were all covered with wood;
When the cowslip and primrose sprang up at my feet;
When the shade of my boughs formed a grateful retreat;
When my leaves were the greenest, my limbs stout and
        strong,
And the birds made my branches a bower of song.
Oft beneath my broad shade hath the light-footed deer
Found a shelter when drowsy, till, startled by fear,
He would dash through the covert t' escape the fleet hound,
While the horn of the hunter re-echoed around.
Over hill and through dale I have viewed, with delight,
The wild chase, till the scene grew be-dimmed to the sight;
Then each leaf-stirring blast had no terror for me —
I was King of the Forest — all around me was free!

F

II.

One midnight, when darkness had shrouded the sky,
When elements warred, and sleet drifted by;
When each cloud, big with anger, rolled over my head,
And Nature seemed striving to waken the dead;
Each flower bowed its head to escape the rude blast,
Each bird crouched with fear as the storm hurried past,
Each bough full of life creaked again and again,
While the wind froze my sap as it ran through each vein.
'Mid the terror and gloom of this terrible night,
At my feet stood the hunter, who, pale with affright,
Sought my boughs, not for safety, for succour, nor shade,
As he'd oft done before while pacing the glade—
His object of search 'mid the elements' strife,
Was death, when all Nature was cringing for life;
And as eager as drowning men struggle for breath,
The hunter sought refuge and quiet in death.
With frenzy-strung nerves he engrasps me around,
With brain changed to fire he springs from the ground,
Till, at length, 'mid my branches, he's dangling high,
And sinks into hell as he climbed to the sky;
While a loud peal of thunder, bursting o'erhead,
Seemed Nature's dread requiem over the dead

HERNE'S OAK.

The learned seek me out as I stand here alone,
A memento of actions in ages agone ,
When the fattest of calves i' the forest was found,
Adorned with a buck's head and fairies around ;
And each child as he passes beholds me with dread,
While each timid mind pictures rude ghosts of the dead.
My beauty hath faded, no flower at my feet,
No wide-spreading branches, no shady retreat ;
All those friends of my youth have long gone to decay,
And I feel that life's tide is fast ebbing away

BRUSH THE TEARS FROM THY CHEEK, LOVE.

I.

Brush the tears from thy cheek, love, for Sorrow and Sadness
  Are exiled to-morrow from this spot of earth ;
The bold invitation of Folly and Madness
  Alone could have brought the false jades to our hearth.
A true angel's whisper breathes softly, " Earth's rudeness
  Is only the mask of a well-dowered queen,
Who will feed thee, absolve thee, and cover thy nudeness,
  Whenever she puts on her mantle of green."

II.

Could not Pity, Compassion, nor Conscience have staid me,
  By appealing to Reason, alas ! I had none ;
They torture me now, as they rise to upbraid me,
  I answer them all with a sigh and a groan.
Come Wisdom, come Valour, and dry up my sorrow,
  Come Hope, with thy blue eyes, and cheer me awhile ;
The crown of my manhood I'll pluck down to-morrow,
  And new joys shall freshen thy half-withered smile.

GIVE ME A THOUSAND WARRIORS.

I.

" Give me a thousand warriors bold,
    A thousand firm and fearless men,
And I will win their weight in gold
    Before I turn me back again.
The city standing by the sea,
    Whose princely merchants stiffly bow,
Shall bribe me with an argosy.
    Or scattered lay in ruins low."

II.

" Give me," another cried, " the moor,
    The deep morass, the kindred fen,
Of labour's weapons just four score,
    And just four score of willing men ;
And I will bring thee riches, too,
    And rob no man, and injure none,
And though I lay no city low,
    A worthier prize shall still be won."

III.

The old Chief, fighting hard with Death,
  Who spoke with pain each heartfelt word,
Said earnestly, with bated breath,
  " When young I trusted to the sword ;
But I have found that every foe
  I slew upon the battle plain,
Retains the power to work me woe
  And charge my cup of bliss with pain.

IV.

" Bring spearhead, haft, and scimitar,
  My good steel bow and stout sword blade,
Bring javelin and bolt of war,
  And they shall furnish pick and spade.
This day, my son, commissioned be
  As captain of a peaceful band,
Bear high the flag of Industry,
  And win fresh trophies from the land."

THE STORY OF SAINT BRIDGET.

I.

Young Bridget was blessed with a sweet pretty face,
Every turn of her limb was ethereal grace,
    And of lovers she had full a score ;
Her foot was the swiftest that ever was seen,
Her parents were peasants—but she was a queen,
    Though no regal vesture she wore.

II.

Young Bridget was sighed for by many a lord,
And world-famous warriors swore by their sword
    That Bridget should soon be their bride ;
They came from the East, they came from the West,
They made her confessor—and each one confessed
    That on earth he loved nothing beside.

III.

"My wealth in broad land shall be yours," cried an earl;
The warrior exclaimed, "Take my sword for a curl,"
     And cast by his buckler and spur;
While a prince of the true Merovignian blood,
No longer on titles nor dignity stood—
     Bowed down like a menial to her.

IV.

"Begone, ye vile tempters," the maiden would say,
And then to her God most devotedly pray
     To shield her from love and from harm;
"Take the rose from my cheek, the fire from mine eye,
The pearl from my mouth, my tresses deep dye,
     And rob me of every charm.

V.

Hear my prayer," she exclaimed, and repeated each word
With a strange winning fervour Devotion had stirred,
     "And fail not to grant my request;
Do not spare me a grace, a treasure, or charm,"
And then she would sit with the holiest calm
     On her beautiful features impressed.

VI.

One night when the stars had gone out one by one,
As Bridget sat praying aloud and alone,
    And counting her beads through and through,
The angels, in pity, gave heed to her prayer—
Determined all future temptations to spare,
    To a maiden so pious and true.

VII.

One by one every charm from her features was torn,
Till the wreck moved men's sorrow like blight-stricken
    corn;
    But, oh! she was happy within;
No murmur escaped her—she uttered no plaint,
Her suitors were angels, for she was a saint,
    With virtues unspotted by sin!

VIII.

The life left within her was God's from that hour,
The Destroyer of Eden was robbed of his power—
    The Serpent lay battered and bruised.
No longer the Tempter temptation could find,
All trace of her beauty was hid in her mind,
    From all worldly dangers reclused!

IX.

The oaks have long fallen on Curragh's broad lands,
The stream of the Liffey is narrowed by sands;
    Yet Bridget's rare virtues still smile :
The daughters of Erin are virtuous and fair,
And true to the lessons they learnt at Kildare
    From Bridget, the Saint of the Isle.

WEEP NOT FOR THE PAST.

I.

Boast ye no more of the pride of past ages,
  Nought's hid in oblivion to call forth your sorrow ;
Let lore-mongers revel in blood-enstained pages,
  Our goal's in the future—our haven to-morrow !
Never look back to discover completeness,
  Search not for life in the dust of the tomb ;
The flowers of the field have lost none of their sweetness,
  Perfection lies hid in Futurity's womb.

II.

She who looked backward and wept for Gomorrah
  Was cursed by her God for the sin she had done ;
Then why over cities and monuments sorrow,
  When grief never raised nor fashioned a stone ?
Call back the past and you call back its errors,—
  Ev'ry step that's been trodden 'tis false to retread ;
Think of its madness, its crimes, and its terrors,
  And work for the living—not weep for the dead !

III.

The deep-planted seed may seem perished and rotten,
    Yet it waits but the sunshine and warm summer rain!
The good and the fruitful shall ne'er be forgotten,
    While the parent seed lives in its offspring again ;
The bright Land of Promise lies onward and sunward,
    By Pisgah's high summit still hid from our sight ;
With a sureness of victory, hasten ye onward,
    The gloomiest hour is pregnant with light.

INVOCATIONS.

I.

"Pray for me, mother, when I am dead,"
  Were the last words she utteréd;
  And the mother knelt ere the night had come,
  And the prayer was heard though her lips were dumb.

II.

"Pray for me, mother, when I am gone,
  For every worldly task undone,"
  And a maiden knelt at a corse's side,
  And prayed for her lover at eventide.

III.

"Pray for me, mother," said a voice at sea,
  When a bark was filling rapidly;
  And the winds bore the tones to a mother's ear,
  And the stillness of night was broken by prayer.

IV.

" Pray for me, courtiers," said a kingly tongue
When I am numbered tho dead among ;
But one by one they stole away,
And those who had flattered forgot to pray.

V.

" Pray for me, kindred," the rich man said,
" When I am borne to my cold earth bed ;"
They heard his prayer with a ready ear,
And smiling—frowning—forgot the prayer.

VI.

The fair child sleeps in a lone graveyard,
Where the new earth rises above the sward,
The lover rests 'neath yon old yew tree,
And the sailor boy in the deep, deep sea ;
Without a mark, without a stone,
Yet God has marked them for his own.

VII.

The king in yon grand mausoleum sleeps,
Where Pity in chiselled marble weeps,
And the rich man rests in yon guarded vault—
" Without a crime—without a fault."

HARVEST HOME.

I.

" The custom, Dame, shall never die
    While I'm controller here :
The master with his servants all
    Should mingle once a year :
And, somehow, I've a notion, Dame,
    That, as old customs change,
The sympathy of English hearts
    Is narrowed in its range.
Go, broach the best October, Dame,
    Prepare to lead the ball,
And I will to the village hie,
    And welcome one and all."

II.

The good old dame, though near three score,
    Made answer to her lord :
" Ay, that I will, with all my heart,
    Just take my honest word.

But stay, before thou goest, man,
  One truth I must instil,
An honest man worn out with toil,
  Should be remembered still :
So mind the shepherd old and lame,
  Mind Jenny at the mill."
" Well done," the farmer laughed and said,
  " By God's help, so I will.

III.

" Come, Jock, fetch Dobbin to the door,
  Then to the cellar go,
And fill a keg of good brown beer,
  'Twill ease their hearts of woe ;
And mind, if thou art honest, lad,
  Like Jenny by the mill,
Shouldst thou grow sick at harvest home,
  Thou'lt be remembered still."
The old dame broached the noblest cask,
  He welcomed one and all ;
And you shall hear when next we meet
  Who led the harvest ball.

OH, DO NOT HASTE AWAY, MY LOVE.

I.

The nightingale's delicious song
  Rings loudly through the wildwood;
The whispering leaves we roam among
  Are joyous in their childhood;
Then do not haste away, my love,
  'Tis long ere evening closes;
We'll sit and listen to the dove,
  And breathe the breath of roses.

II.

The blossoms of the hawthorn bough,
  The white bloom of the cherry,
The flowering gorse, the blooming sloe,
  With beauty bid us tarry:
Then do not haste away, my love,
  'Tis long ere evening closes;
We'll sit and listen to the dove,
  And breathe the breath of roses.

III.

Oh, who would quit such scenes as these,
   For all the town possesses,
When we can sit beneath the trees
   And feast ourselves with kisses?
Then, do not haste away, my love,
   'Tis long ere evening closes;
But sit and listen to the dove,
   And breathe the breath of roses.

THE ORPHAN GIRL OF BRITTANY.

I.

"Come tell me, mother, that strange tale
　　You told me yester eve,
　About that little orphan girl
　　They christened Genevieve;
　For I would store in Memory's urn
　　The story of her woes,
　And imitate her gentle life,
　　Unmindful of its close."

II.

" A fair-haired child of Brittany "—
　　The mother thus began,
" The fairy-featured daughter
　　Of a poor, yet honest man,
　Was straying through the woods one day,
　　As children oft will stray,
　Neglectful of the beaten track
　　That marked the trodden way.

III.

" She wandered here, she wandered there,
　　Led on by something new—
The song of birds, the ripe wild fruit
　　That in profusion grew :
The wildings scattered round her feet,
　　And foxgloves white and red,
And the whispers of the many leaves
　　That hung around her head.

IV.

" A squirrel leapt from bough to bough,
　　A wild bee passed along,
And then a thousand merry flies
　　All mad with dance and song :
A spider's web hung o'er her way,
　　With beads of pearly dew,—
Beguiled thus, the child forgot
　　How swift the hours flew.

V.

" Then came that silent, solemn hour,
　　The gloaming of the day,
That tells us all that's beautiful
　　Is doomed to pass away,

And whispered to the truant child
    By vagrant fancies led,
' Mark how the swift-winged clouds of night
    Are gathering round your head.'

VI.

" But, ah! too late : the warning came,
    For one who did not know,
And, in her pathless wanderings,
    Kept pacing to and fro,
And to whose earnest, prayerful words,
    Each echo answered back,
The very words she spoke aloud—
    ' Is this the homeward track?'

VII.

" A glow-worm, creeping through the grass,
    Threw forth its feeble light,
Just strong enough to free its world
    From danger and from night ;
A few dim stars were in the heavens,
    But these she could not see,
For the over-hanging branches
    That spread from tree to tree.

VIII.

" Her father searched the whole house through—
    Then searched it o'er again,
And, shouting, ran through wood and field,
    And down the long green lane.   .
' Sweet Genevieve, come back to me,
    Come back, thou spotless one ;
Where art thou, angel of my house ?
    Oh, leave me not alone !'

IX.

" The night sped on, and Genevieve
    O'ertired, lay down to rest
Beneath a spreading hawthorn bush,
    Where linnets built their nest ;
And there she lay till early morn,
    Nor dreamed, nor thought of wrong,
Till wakened from her slumbers
    By their sleep-dispelling song.

X.

" ' What fairy work is this ?' she cried,
    And gently raised her head,
' Where are the curtains mother wove
    And hung around my bed,—

With all their pretty pencillings
  Of bushes, trees, and flowers?
They surely have not blossomed thus
  In these few silent hours!

XI.

" ' Who taught her pencilled birds to sing—
  Her flowers to shed perfume;
And made a fairies' palace
  Of my unpretending room?
Oh! father, oh! whence all this change
  My wondering eyes descry?
My little window's grown so large
  It lets in all the sky!'

XII.

" And as she drew her little hand
  Across her troubled brow,—
' My chamber walls have grown so wide
  I cannot see them now!
Oh! father, dear! where art thou gone?'
  The little maiden cried;
' Oh! father, dear! where art thou gone?'
  The echoing woods replied.

XIII.

"'Come, Memory, come, arouse thyself!'
      Said Pity, hovering near;
  'I would not have so fair a brow
      Such signs of sorrow wear;
  Exert the powers within thy keep
      And grant her soul relief:
  Thou wouldst not see a face so fair
      Despoiled by Doubt and Grief?'

XIV.

"'The clouds like shadows pass away
      That hung around her brow,'
  Said Pity—'and her mild blue eyes
      Are lit by sunshine now—
  Behold, how Heaven receives the gifts
      The poor and humble give!
  The song from out the hawthorn bus'
      The prayer from Genevieve!'

SECOND NIGHT.

I.

" She wandered forth in search of home,
    Through many a wooded dell—
As ancient dames in Brittany
    On winter evenings tell—
Through many a leafy wilderness,
    Down many a heathery strath ;
But Fancy, like a will-o'-th'-wisp,
    Aye drew her from the path.

II.

" With sunny features stained with dyes
    Of blackberry and sloe,
She sat beside a forest spring
    And watched its waters flow ;
Just like a little Zingaree,
    Neglected and forlorn ;
Her arms by cruel brambles rent,
    Her little frock all torn.

III.

"Oh! who shall picture all the woe
　　Her only parent felt,
As wrapt, in one long, earnest prayer
　　From night till morn he knelt?
How 'neath the burning sun of noon
　　He sought her mother's grave,
And called on her to intercede
　　That Heaven her child might save

IV.

"Her pockets filled with hazel nuts
　　By summer sun made brown,
And by her side the hookéd stick
　　That pulled the branches down,
With hop-bine, and wild briony
　　Entwined about her hair,
No canvas in the world e'er held
　　A picture half so fair!

V.

"The windings of a hunter's horn
　　Broke through the leafy glade,
And lithesome as a startled deer,
　　Up leapt the little maid;

Then rushing on with heedless haste
    O'er many a fallen tree,
She heard the wild wood echo back
    Loud shouts of victory.

VI.

" An antlered deer with haunches torn,
    And dropping crimson gore,
A wide and square-built serving man
    On thick-set shoulders bore ;
And round his feet, fierce eager dogs,
    Made wood and welkin ring;
While steadily behind them rode
    The courtiers of the king!

VII.

'Then riding forth on foaming steed
    From out the tangled brake,
A man with high and haughty mien
    Close followed in their wake ;
Next rode a slender courtly youth,
    With long and flowing hair ;
.nd, following fast, poor Genevieve
    Came running in the rear.

VIII.

" All dripping wet with morning dew,
 And flushed and out of breath,
And like a streamer in the wind
 Her newly woven-wreath :
' Oh! Sir,' she cried, ' take pity, pray !
 And leave me not alone ;
Oh, Sir !'—and down the maiden fell,
 As lifeless as a stone.

IX.

" The stirrups now like cymbals clash,
 The saddle seems on fire,
While Genevieve is gently raised
 From out the slush and mire ;
And then the shout for help was heard,
 And courtiers flocked around,
And Genevieve, with wondrous care,
 Unto the steed was bound.

X.

" Once more the cortege moves along,
 In all its courtly pride,
And foremost walks the serving man
 With shoulders strong and wide ;

And next the mounted courtiers pass
    With measured step, and slow ;
And then the stern-faced monarch rides
    With deep and wrinkled brow :

XI.

" Last, closely following, came the prince,
    The idol of the land ;
The bridle of his Arab steed
    Grasped firmly in his hand :
And as they slowly wound along
    Through many a wooded glen,
The sun sank down behind the hill,
    And hid its face from men.

XII.

" And now, within the shadows
    Of a castle old and grey,
They gather in the misty light
    That closes in the day :
The bell is rung, the gate withdrawn,
    And rushing here and there,
Are seen the lusty servitors,
    With heads and arms all bare.

XIII.

" The steeds are to their stables led,
　　The hounds their kennel seek,
And Genevieve is borne along,
　　With fainting form and weak,
Through many a long, dark corridor,
　　Through vestibule and hall ;
And she, the object of their care,
　　Unmindful of it all !

XIV.

' For many a weary day and night,
　　By fever stricken dumb,
Poor simple-minded Genevieve
　　Lay in her little room ;
At length, with each revolving sun,
　　Her strength returned anew,
And the roses painted on her cheeks
　　Regained their crimson hue.

XV.

" ' Oh, take me to my dear old home,
　　And let me see once more
My only parent, rich in love,
　　And yet, alas! how poor!

Though absent, all his treasured love
  Will only fiercer burn,
And he will surely die of grief,
  If I should not return.'

XVI.

" Her prayer was heard by one whose heart
  Such tales of dolour moved ;
For he had sighed for absent scenes,
  And still the absent loved :
So, side by side, at autumn's fall,
  When all the trees were bare,
They jointly sought her father's cot —
  Alas! he was not there !

XVII.

" In vain he struck the oaken door—
  In vain he waited long ;
And vainly, to allay her fears,
  He whistled, laughed, and sung ;
At length the stubborn door gave way :
  But nothing could they find,
Save signs of long, long absence,
  To rack her troubled mind.

XVIII.

" Her doll was lying on the shelf,
  Her hoop hung on the wall,
And dust through many a crevice blown,
  Had settled down on all ;
Her Sunday frock, her bran-new shoes,
  And—source of many joys—
The little box her father made
  To hold her treasured toys.

XIX.

" The clock's once faithful pendulum
  Had long since ceased to swing ;
The linnet, that she loved so much,
  Had lost its power to sing ;
The old arm chair was tenantless,
  The flowers— all were dead ;
And every thought the scene awoke
  To Death and Sorrow led.

XX.

" ' Oh, heaven !' she cried, ' have pity, pray !
  On one so weak and lone ;
The only friend I had on earth
  For evermore has gone ;

No loving words will come again
　　My wayward heart to cheer :
Oh, take me from this scene of woe,
　　I cannot linger here.'

XXI.

" He took her gently by the hand,
　　And, with a brother's love,
The crushing load upon her mind
　　Strove vainly to remove ;
' The ties that bound him to his home
　　Your absence may have broken,
' But, wherefore, say that he is dead,
　　When not a word was spoken ? '

XXII.

" ' Oh, woe is me ! ' cried Genevieve,
　　' No tongue could plainer speak ;
And oh ! the bitter, bitter words !
　　My poor, poor heart will break ;
Pray take me to my mother's grave
　　On yonder bleak hill side,
And we shall find her worshipper
　　Is resting by her side.

XXIII.

"'Oh! cease to tell me that he lives
    All doubts are now at rest;
Another landmark for the dead
    Is stretching East and West.'
Adown her cheeks the hot tears ran
    Like water from a spring,
Then, like a wounded bird she fell,
    When stricken on the wing.

I.

"The tide of time rolls ever on,
　　No stubborn rocks assail;
It does not linger with the calm,
　　Nor quicken with the gale;
It does not mock the swift-winged bird,
　　And then the tortoise slow,
The calm and endless tide of Time
　　Is equal in its flow.

II.

"Within a crimson-curtained room,
　　Two hundred years agone,
A comely maiden weeping sat,
　　With Sorrow, all alone:
She wore the courtly robes of pride,
　　The trappings of a queen;
But stateliness and dignity
　　Were nowhere to be seen.

III.

"She was the self-same Genevieve
  I pictured—young and fair,
With mild blue eyes, and crimson cheeks,
  And golden-tinted hair;
The flower of the blushing rose,
  The mid-day of the morn;
With all her first-blown loveliness
  Unspotted and unshorn.

IV.

"'The threatened woe has come at last,
  The babbler's tongue has spoken;
And that brief spell of happiness
  For evermore is broken;
My princely love is borne away,
  And I am left to mourn;
A weeper in a troubled world,
  Unpitied and forlorn.'

V.

"Thus wailed the gentle Genevieve,
  For, oh, she knew full well
The meaning of those few sad words
  That broke her happy spell;

She knew their love had been betrayed
  By one whose envious wrath
Was like the hot wind of the East,
  The trumpet sound of death.

VI.

" For many a weary day and night
  She listened for the voice,
Whose whispered words of love and truth
  Made heart and soul rejoice ;
But not a sound from those sweet lips
  Whose music kindled love,
E'er fell upon her listening ear,
  Wherever she might rove.

VII.

" The skylark and the nightingale, ·
  The linnet and the thrush,
And all the little chorestors
  That dwelt in tree and bush,
Sang sweetly to her day by day,
  In wondrous accord,
And tried to chase from memory,
  The presence of her lord.

VIII.

"A year passed, and no tidings came,
    Save that which gossips told,
Whose tales were truly balls of snow,
    That gathered as they rolled,
Till, melted in the warmth of truth,
    (As snow returns to rain),
To what they were, till crystallised
    To please the weak and vain.

IX.

"But hers was not a simple grief,
    That gossips could relieve,
But one that twined around the heart,
    Of hapless Genevieve :
It was no ranting, loud-mouth'd woe,
    That frights you with its stare,
But one whose sting is deadlier far,
    And poisons with a tear.

X.

"'Twas on a merry Christmas morn,
    The Christmas logs were burning,
When tidings through the castle spread,
    'Prince Edward is returning,'

And then the king in haste appeared,
  And summoned those he trusted,
And bade them get their armour on,
  That long had lain by rusted.

XI.

"The fire of wrath re-lit his eye,
  That age had robbed of lustre,
As he beheld his warlike crew
  Within the court-yard muster.
' Let yonder drawbridge be upraised,
  Arm, arm, each fort and tower ;
Then march direct to St. Brieux,
  And test Rebellion's power.'

XII.

" 'Twas thus the stern-faced monarch spoke,
  And ere an hour was passed,
The bannerets of Brittany
  Were waving in the blast :
That noon a deadly fight was fought,
  And Edward won the day,
While the stern old king of Brittany
  Was slaughtered in the fray.

XIII.

" At length the conquering host appeared
 Before the castle walls ;
' I summon all to yield to me ! '
 Their favoured chieftain calls ;
' I never yet betrayed a trust,'
 The captain cried within,
 And will not yield an inch to thee,
 Save that which thou can'st win.'

XIV.

" The conflict raged most furiously,
 And hearts were filled with ire,
Till, from the castle's western walls,
 Arose a streak of fire,
That broadened as the moments flew,
 And hissed and roared amain,
Telling the trusted servants all
 Resistance was in vain.

XV.

" The gates were quickly flung aside,
 The bridges flung across ;
And men in safety walked above
 The deep and yawning foss ;

And foremost in the crowd was seen
   Young Edward rushing on,
With eager cries of 'Follow me!
   The crowning deed's undone!'

XVI.

"On, on, he rushed, led on by Love,
   The western tower to win;
For he had heard that Genevieve
   Was perishing within;
O'er blackened rafter, girt by flame,
   Through passages of smoke,
O'er scorching floors, with heat athirst,
   His speed no peril broke.

XVII.

"What balm shall soothe his troubled soul?
   What worldly wealth atone?
The empire of his heart was lost,
   He walked the world alone!
A people's love was nought to hers,
   And riches—what are they?
The glittering chains of human hearts,
   The baubles of a day.

XVIII.

"Such is the tale of Genevieve,
  As it was told to me,
By one who treasured it for years
  Within her memory :
From her to me, from me to you,
  From you to some dear friend :
Thus simple tales of honest worth
  May journey without end.

XIX.

" We little know how words may roll
  Adown the stream of time ;
There's many rolling, rolling yet,
  That started in earth's prime :
So they be virtuous, let them roll,
  Like boulders down a river,
They'll polish as they pass along,
  Then, starlike, shine for ever."

THE CORN AND THE POPPY.

I.

THE poppy may raise its haughty head,
  With its crimson robe of scorn ;
But is it not from the same earth fed
  As the unpretending corn ?
Does it not crave for the heavenly dew,
  And drink of the living shower ?
Then why be so proud of its blood-red hue,
  When its glory will last but an hour ?

II.

Does the slothful liquid in every pore
  Breed pride so rank and so base ?
And the poppy dream that the earth's wide floor
  Was made for its slumb'rous race ?
The corn by its side shall be dressed in gold,
  Ere the summer has passed away,
And its wealth be greater and richer threefold,
  When the reaper shall pass this way.

III.

The blast of heaven, or the lightning's dart,
  May slay every poppy on earth ;
But who would weep, or, affrighted start
  At vain phantoms of famine and dearth ?
The sun would shine and the rich rain fall
  Though each poppy had passed away,
And the Earth would feast her children all,
  To-morrow, as well as to-day.

A DREAM IN THE RUINS.

I.

I HAD wandered far, when a ruin old
   Threw its shapeless shadows across my way;
And I thought what mysteries it might unfold!
   As it stood, time-crowned, in the gear of decay.

II.

I secretly crept through a low-shattered wall,
   And wandered among the long, rank grass,
Gazing with awe at each battlement tall,
   That frowned like a giant upon the dwarfed mass:

III.

The wind gave a shriek as it rushed by the scene,
   The rays of the moon through each cleft stone had darted,
And I sat myself down, like a lone eastern queen,
   And wept for the grandeur of glories departed.

IV.

I was drugged with fatigue, and I soon fell asleep,
    With a stone for my pillow, the earth for my bed;
I dreamt I lay fast in the castle's fell keep,
    Where all hope of succour for ever had fled,

V.

Where the chain that once bound me lay broken and rusted,
    And the strong iron window through which I'd been fed;
With blood and the tears of mine eyes was encrusted,
    And I sighed for the portal that leads to the dead.

VI.

The shriek of the night-bat, the croak of the raven,
    In the passing of years grew endearing to me,
And my name on the walls was a hundred times graven,
    For I thought it might thus be preserved to the free!

VII.

I dreamt that my crime was a crime unforgiven,
    While a throne cursed the world, or a tyrant drew breath:
I had sworn to live free in the sunlight of Heaven,
    And had raised the proud standard of "Freedom or Death."

VIII.

In highlands and lowlands men heard the proud story,
　And thousands of brave hearts in unison came ;
And we purchased, with daring, fair freedom and glory,
　Till the lords of the earth grew alarmed at my fame.

IX.

We banded together !　As freemen undaunted,
　With truth in our hearts and stripp'd swords in our hands,
We rushed on the foe !　My life seemed enchanted,
　As reapers in harvest we swept the broad lands ;

X.

Out-numbered and slain were the dear friends that loved me,
　I fell 'neath the force of a treacherous blow !
And at night from the field, bound in chains, they removed
　　me,
　While the Heavens wept in pity at Freedom's o'erthrow.

XI.

I awoke ! and the vision still clung to my brain !
　I sought out the keep with a feverish tread ;
And bore off as relics the staple and chain
　Which lay on the ground 'mid the bones of the dead !

THE PRIDE OF THE HOMESTEAD.

I.

When storms have stripped the mountain,
   I have seen the old dun cow,
With an instinct quite bewitching,
   Seek the sheltered lands below :
For she loves to hear the music,
   From the treble weak and slim,
To the loud and sonorous bass that tells
   Her milk has reached the brim.

    So we'll bless the honest cow
      For befriending high and low,
    May she never want for fodder
      While the hand of man can sow.

II.

You may milk her in the evening,
   And then go to bed and dream ;
But there's magic in the dairy,
   And her milk will change to cream.

Ay, there's gold upon its surface,
   While there's wealth in all below :
The richest stream throughout the land,
   Is that which leaves the cow.

         So we'll bless the honest cow
            For befriending high and low,
         May she never want for fodder,
            While the hand of man can sow.

                    III

When our first-born, weak and ailing,
   Turned his wee mouth from my breast,
How I trembled for his safety,
   And sought succour from the beast !
And she gave it quick and willing,
   When my babe was like to die,
For her udder's like the fountain,
   You cannot milk it dry.

         So we'll bless the honest cow
            For befriending high and low,
         May she never want for fodder
            While the hand of man can sow.

IV.

She has nourished us in winter,
    When the snow lay thick around,
And the plants died in their cradle,
    On the unprotected ground ;
She has nourished us in summer,
    When the rain refused to fall,
And she never deigns to loiter
    When she hears the milkmaid call.

        So we'll bless the honest cow
            For befriending high and low,
        May she never want for fodder
            While the hand of man can sow.

ON THE RUINS OF READING ABBEY.

I.

Thou art far more than the sepulchre
    Of a dark and worn-out creed,
Thou long-wrecked home of learning,
    And of saints whom death has freed.

II.

Who, listless to the strife without,
    In solemn silence wrought,
And garnered the rich fragments
    Of an infant nation's thought.

III.

Full many a kingly-thoughted mind
    Our ancient vessels bore,
From many an eastern nation
    T'' illume this darkened shore ;

IV.

But still 'twas thine own shaven crowns
  These kindred spirits sought,
Who paid the wanderers back in kind
  For golden treasures brought.

V.

When rude hands spoiled thine altars,
  When thy chambers echoed oaths,
They might have spared thy treasures,
  The Vandals and the Goths;

VI.

They might have saved from flame and wrack
  Those treasures of the mind,
And left untouched the heirlooms
  Of unlettered human kind.

VII.

I know thou taught'st an iron creed
  In those benighted days;
That many a sainted fosman died
  'Mid faggots all a-blaze:

VIII.

And in thy dismal dungeons,
  Where day was never seen;
That many a God-like spirit sank
  'Neath torture sharp and keen;

IX.

But thy goodness is undying,
  And thine evil passed away,
Like a cloud before the summer sun,
  And night before the day!

A BALLAD.

I.

LISTEN to me, a story I'll tell
 Of an old dame withered and grey,
Who used in a neat little cottage to dwell
 By the side of the river Tay.
The old dame's pride was her children three,
 Three jolly boys, I trow,
For they kept their mother from poverty
 By help of the spade and plough.

II.

" Alas ! " one day, the old dame cried,
 " The staff of mine age has gone ;
Fortune has stolen a mother's pride,
 And left me to weep alone.
Three worthier sons no mother could find
 Throughout the live-long day,"
And the old dame wept till her eyes went blind
 As they sailed from the River Tay.

III.

Three jolly, roaring, soldier lads,
 Are coming over the sea;
The blood of brave foemen dims their blades,
 They are her children three.
"Ho! Mother?" they shout, far up the hill,
 " We'll cheer your heart this day!"
But the soldiers' tears helped to turn the mill,
 That stood on the River Tay.

LIFE AND DEATH.

I.

THE rich ore's found 'neath the buried rock,
  The pearl in the deep blue sea,
Which only the daring hand may clutch,
  Or the daring eye may see.

II.

The lily bud may waken thought,
  But deeper thought will spring,
From the lily dead and the empty clay,
  When the soul has taken wing.

III.

Each grave is a casket of rich, rare thought,
  Which fools alone despise;
A legacy rich, when homeward called,
  The dead have flung to the wise;

IV.

And sermons are spoken by dead, cold lips,
   Which breathing lips never spoke ;
As the stately column in all its pride,
   Says less than the column broke.

V.

Then come with me from earth's gayest scenes,
   The roar of life's rude waves,
And we'll return with our lives enriched
   With the spoil of dead men's graves.

A ROUND OF LOVE.

I.

THE squirrel loves the hazel tree,
    The swine the stalwart oak ;
The silkworm loves the mulberry,
    The bee the hollyhock ;
The butterfly the clover leaf,
    The wren the hawthorn bush ;
The sparrow loves the harvest sheaf,
    The mistle charms the thrush.

II.

I love the fruity hazel tree,
    The emblematic oak ;
The rich and juicy mulberry,
    The bright-hued hollyhock ;
I love the triple-clover leaf,
    The flowering hawthorn bough ;
The richly-dowered golden sheaf,
    The bright-eyed mistletoe.

HURRAH! FOR THE BRAVE.

I.

Come, Landlord, and bring me a bowl of the best,
   For I mean to be merry to-day;
Ere the sun that's now rising sinks down in the west,
   Dull Care shall be far, far away.
There are ills in this life, but outbrave them, my boys,
   And never desparingly yield,
For the soldier who shrinks in the battle of life,
   Is not worth a curse in the field!

Hurrah! for the brave! in the battle of life!
   Hurrah! boys, hurrah! for the brave.

II.

I'm a soldier of fortune, with nothing to lose,
   Still I never was given to strife;
I have drubbed all the rough-fisted foes I have met
   In the ceaseless encounters of life;

I have fought with Disease, I have struggled with Want;
   I've been wounded, but comrades, what then?
If they come, boys, to-morrow, and tempt me to fight,
   I have faith I shall conquer again.
Hurrah! for the brave! in the battle of life!
   Hurrah! boys, hurrah! for the brave!

III.

Come, Landlord, and bring me a bowl of the best,
   For I mean to be merry to-day;
Ere the sun that's now rising sinks down in the west,
   Dull Care shall be far, far away.
Look alive, I've a merry old heart beating yet,
   And 'twill merrily beat till I die;
But, mark me, dull prating still leaves one a-thirst,
   Bring the bowl, while in chorus we cry—
Hurrah! for the brave! in the battle of life!
   Hurrah! boys, hurrah! for the brave!

FALSE BRAVERY.

I.

As childhood dies, and manhood takes its place,
 We often deem our independence won ;
But, whence the mask we wear upon our face ?
 Oh, rather has not servitude begun ?
The child, in sorrow, will not hide its tears,
While griefs suppressed proclaim men's growing fears.

II.

I love not tears, and yet I love not those,
 Who truly boast they never shed a tear ;
They are the outward badges of our woes
 That heaven designed the sorrow-struck should wear :
I do confess, I deem the brave man weak,
Who wears a smile like rouge upon his cheek.

ENGLAND'S GLORY.

I.

Shall I drag the hidden truth to light,
  From the clouded page of story?
And show you the source of England's might—
  The fount of her undimmed glory?
The truth has been cunningly long concealed,
  By men whom the world call sages:
Let the book of truth be now unsealed,
  And the people read from its pages.

  The builders of nations are those who toil,
  The source of their wealth the stubborn soil;
  So shout, boys, shout, till the welkin rings,
  From labour alone true glory springs.

II.

They have told us how England gained by war,
  From what dangers the sword has kept her,
Of the giants who governed her senate and bar,
  And grappled old England's sceptre:

They tell us of cities sacked and won,
   By the ruthless hand of the spoiler,
But where of the glorious deeds long done
   By the kingly, uncrowned toiler?

   The builders of nations are those who toil,
   The source of their wealth the stubborn soil;
   So shout, boys, shout, till the welkin rings,
   From labour alone true glory springs.

III.

True history shall be written yet,
   When the deeds of all, unfolded,
Shall be read aloud to the nations met
   To hear how the world was moulded:
And none, in vain, search a thousand leaves
   For the truth shall lay before us,
In a song that a bard of labour weaves,
   While the people swell its chorus.

   The builders of nations are those who toil,
   The source of their wealth the stubborn soil;
   So shout, boys, shout, till the welkin rings,
   From labour alone true glory springs.

THE RUINED TOWER.

I.

A WATCH-TOWER stood on yonder mountain's brow
  A century past—those ruins mark the spot ;
Go, ye, who would a mighty lesson know,
  And mark its time-worn relics as they rot.
Behold how moss and lichen share the spoil,
  The soulless plund'rors of Time's vanquished prey ;
The trailing ivy how it clingeth still,
  And gains more life where most is found decay.

II.

Learn how the higher rests upon the lower,
  How lowest fates the highest may control ;
How one decaying stone may sap a tower,
  How many ones combine to form a whole.
The topmost stone, hurled down the mountain side,
  Lying lower, deeper sunken, than its brother,
May teach the vaunting nothingness of Pride,
  And bid us pause ere yet we slight another.

III.

As baseness thrives on virtues, long since dead,
   And claims a kingdom that immortals won,
So slimy reptiles, putrefaction-fed,
   Revel where once the eagle built his throne.
See death and life inseparably woven:
   Disorder—order! chaos re-arranged!
See indestruction by destruction proven,
   And form for form, and life for life exchanged!

THE FIELD OF BALAKLAVA.

1.

Here stood the brave sons of a chivalrous race,
  Whose deed are immortal in story ;
And here with the foemen they fought face to face,
  And here they fell covered with glory !
The green grass and flowers that garland the plain,
  Point out where the battle grew thicker—
And the thirsty soil drank the blood of brave men,
  As a Bacchanal quaffeth good liquor.

II.

'Tis God's acre wo tread—let your foot press with care,
  For beneath are the sheaves of Death's harvest ;
While the wild flowers blooming are monuments fair,
  To mark out the tombs of the bravest.
Tears fell like the rain on each rude-fashioned grave,
  At the wreck of their pride and their powers ;
But the life that once kindled the hearts of the brave,
  Now smiles upon heaven through the flowers.

III.

When we first read the tale by our own fireside,
    With its fierceness and daring bewildering;
Our fathers' stout hearts were near bursting with pride,
    While our mothers shed tears for their children.
We marvelled how men fought as gods fought of old,
    And we lavished our praise without sparing;
And proudly compared it to Marathon's field,
    With its courage and deeds of high daring.

IV.

On this flower-clad spot one brother lay low—
    There was blood on his long silken tresses—
But Right had not nerved the strong arm of the foe,
    And the pride of his presence still blesses:
But one ne'er returned to the home of his birth,
    And his tongue ne'er shall tell the proud story,
How he fought for the fame of his own mother earth,
    While the bride of his heart was her Glory.

THE SHOEMAKER'S LINNET.

I.

Cheer of my desolate garret,
　　Why art thou loath to depart?
Hast thou beheld the big sorrow
　　Fate has entwined round my heart?
Why dost thou hover around me,
　　And perch on thine own prison door?
My friends, one by one, have long left me,
　　The poor only think of the poor.

II.

Cheer of my desolate garret,
　　Rich in thy dower of song,
Fly, fly, to the welcoming bower,
　　And join the gay warbling throng.
Why should I chain thee to lighten
　　The woes I am bound to endure?
Go, go, to the rich-tinted woodland,
　　The poor only think of the poor.

III.

How strange that a bird should befriend me,
   Wh n brothers cast friendship away;
'Tis friendship alone could detain thee,
   From courting the white-blossomed May.
Then stay, and a blythe song shall cheer us;
   Thy music, Heaven's music, out-pour;
And I'll treat thee as thou wert an angel
   That Heaven sent to comfort the poor.

THE RIGHT AND THE WRONG.

I.

He cannot err who wars with Hate and Strife,
　And braves the scorn of every fool and knave,
Who dares to lead an honest, sober life,
　And loathes alike the tyrant and the slave;
Nor he who, sworn to live and die by Truth,
　Diggeth his grave in consecrated ground;
Nor he who gives his manhood and his youth
　To scatter hope where vice and fear abound.

II.

The man who errs is he who lives a slave—
　Who sinks the Future in the dying Now;
Who sells his soul to every soulless knave,
　And brandeth "Slavery" on a brother's brow;
'Tis he who speaketh of a heaven above,
　Forgetful of the sinful life he leads;
Who preacheth ever of a Saviour's love,
　And scatters seeds of strife where'er he treads:

III.

'Tis he who, catching at the bubble fame,
    Has stooped beneath the level of his race ;
Or, lost to Virtue, takes her honoured name
    To blot his sins, and save him from disgrace ;
'Tis he who, knowing Truth, dares truth to mar,
    Or, knowing Flattery, courts her poisonous breath ;
Who cries out " Peace !" if peace be smouldering war,
    Or lifts the crimson standard for a wreath.

COME ALL YOU JOLLY PLOUGHMEN.

I.

Come all you jolly ploughmen, of courage stout and bold,
That labour all the winter in stormy winds and cold,

    For to-night we'll merry be,

    Prepare yourselves for jollity !

We'll sing and whistle louder than the winds across the wold.
The harvest has been garnered, and the corn is ripe and
    sound ;

A richer crop was never seen in all the country round ;

You've done your duty bravely, boys, and won me gold
    galore,

So, we'll have a merry making, as our fathers did of yore.

II.

Come all you jolly harvestmen, you're welcome one and all,
The fattest ox the farm could boast is roasting in the hall,

    For to-night we'll merry be,

    Prepare yourselves for jollity,

And bring your scythes and sickles, boys, to decorate the
    wall.

A cask of real old stingo, finely flavoured, rich and strong,

Will wash away each taint of care, and tune your throats

    for song,

And when the barrel's empty, boys, you shall not want for

    more,

For we'll feast ourselves till morning, as our fathers did of

    yore.

III.

Come all who labour on the farm, no matter how or where,

From the ploughboy to the shepherd with his white and

    ⁓ flowing hair,

    For to-night we'll merry be,

    Prepare yourselves for jollity,

And feast and drink, and laugh and sing, without a thought

    of care.

Go, and tell the village parson he is wanted here to-night,

With his free and loving nature, and his passion for the

    right:

And bring your wives and sweethearts, lads, we'll trip it

    o'er the floor;

And keep it up till morning, as our fathers did of yore.

A PHASE OF LIFE.

I.

I HAVE heard men speak of an Eden land,
  Where a thousand flowers are springing;
Where the sky is clear, and the air is pure,
  And a thousand birds are singing;
Of valleys where brooklets flow noiselessly on,
  And mountains that touch the sky;
But nor mountain nor stream, save in a dream,
  Ever gladdened my raptureless eye.

II.

I have heard them speak of the green, green fields,
  And the hedgerows running between them;
But the only glimpse that I ever caught
  Was from dreams or from eyes that had seen them;
And in fancy I trod on the velveted sod,
  Ay, free from the crowded alley,
And with heartfelt pride, climbed the hill's ruggéd side,
  Or followed the stream through the valley.

III.

I have dreamt of a fair-haired shephord boy,
    With his wee pet lamb beside him,
And a dog who never like Judas loved
    His master, and yet denied him :
Of corn sheaves ranged in tho harvest field,
    And the merry reaper-train,
Till I shouted among tho jovial throng,
    And followed the burdened wain.

IV.

'Tis hard to die in this dark, damp cell,
    And know there aro health-giving places,
But harder still to see thousands livo
    With Death written on their faces ;
But who would not dio—no matter how—
    Though cycles before their timo,
Than eke out life in a land of strife
    On bread that is purchased with crime ?

LET YOUR SONGS BE ANGEL SONGS.

I.

Let all your songs be angel songs,
  Nor thought nor word betraying
That truth or love has been defiled,
  Or moral worth decaying;
Where round about each well-clothed thought
  A glorious truth is clinging:
And every man's a better man
  For hearing them or singing.

    And every line shall strip a wrong,
      And lay it bare before us;
    And we shall feel the heart respond,
      When we join in the chorus.

II.

Let all your songs be angel songs,
  That young and old may listen:
With words to cheer the saddest heart
  And make the dull eye glisten:

For there's rare virtue in such songs,
 True joy and comfort bringing ;
And every line's a row of pearls,
 A heaven-born poet's stringing.

  And every line shall strip a wrong,
   And lay it bare before us ;
  And we shall feel the heart respond,
   When we join in the chorus.

III.

Let all your songs be angel songs,
 Where truth and love are spoken ;
A song of triumph when the chain
 Of slavery is broken ;
A song of woe at fitting hour,
 Of love when love shall move us ;
And let this be the live-long day,
 Till all the world shall love us.

  For there's a glory in a song,
   Where lasses join in chorus ;
  And if they love ere we begin
   At ending they'll adore us

THE PATH OF DUTY.

I.

Never depart from the straight line of duty,
  'Tis a sanctified path every angel has trod ;
While the pathway of sin—though it tempt ye with
      beauty—
  Would only decoy ye from freedom and God.
The hills may be steep, but they're covered with glory,
  The rocks may be stubborn and hard to subdue ;
But the brave men who climbed them with feet bruised
    and gory,
  Have shown what true courage and daring can do.

Oh, heed not the tempting of fools wed to folly ;
  Their cries lead to pitfalls—each word is a snare ;
Like the red berry plucked by the child from the holly,
  Their hearts are pierced through, while they dance
    without care.

II.

There's no wanton like Sloth on the face of creation,
  E'en the proudest have perished who bowed to her
    sway;
In her arms we have found the whole strength of a nation,
  Like the frailest of flowers, die out in a day.
There is nothing I trow, that will polish and soften
  Those fierce jutting crags like the traffic of men;
Let their tramp then, like racers, be heard loud and often
  Till the straight line of duty is worn to a plain.

Oh, heed not the temptings of fools wed to folly,
  Their cries lead to pitfalls —each word is a snare;
Like the red berry plucked by the child from the holly,
  Their hearts are pierced through, while they dance
    without care.

HOME.

I.

If I have gloried o'er a nugget found,
   Or thrilled with pride to see my wealth increase,
One simple thought my sole ambition crowned,
   'Twas here to dwell, and close my life in peace.
But like the poor, who grow rich in their sleep,
   And wake to find a dream is all their store,
My visioned scenes are shells cast from the deep,
   Telling of what they were, and nothing more.

II.

The farm neglected—fences broke away;
   The homestead blasted by the breath of time;
Neglect and ruin jointly holding sway,
   Where once Neglect was punished as a crime.
Yon water-wheel, as quiet as the grave,
   No more revolves beneath a miller's care;
High flags and rushes o'er the waters wave,
   And ruin—slothful ruin—everywhere!

III.

What blighting agency has thus betrayed
    The things I loved into such ruthless keep?
I see them now, and, child-like, stand dismayed,
    And turn to leave them, as I turn to weep:
The scattered peasants—whither have they fled?
    Where mighty rivers seek th' Atlantic coast,
Some try their fortunes—others, long since dead;
    While all are far away, and all are lost!

A SONG TO THE CLOUDS.

1.

Gather ye, gather ye, clouds of night,
   Where have ye been all day ?
Scattered abroad by the sun's fierce light,
Want ye the courage to brave the fight,
   And stand in the heated fray ?

II.

Build ye a rampart high and wide,
   Phalanx on phalanx stand,
Reaching to Heaven and based on the tide,
Spanning the air with a giant's stride,
   And guarding all the land.

III.

Press ye as close as the mountains dun,
   Then let your thunders roll,
Ray after ray shall bend its course,
Doubling like bayonets struck with force,
   Against an iron wall.

IV.

Gather ye, gather ye, clouds of night,
  Gather ye thick and fast,
Conquer the sun's fierce burning light,
Why should the tyrant shine so bright,
  In glory unsurpassed ?

V.

Stand on his pathway, bar his track,
  End ye, his long, long reign,
Press ye together, warriors black,
Muster in strength and hurl him back,
  And earth shall be yours again.

THE SONG OF THE DROVER.

Over hill and through valley, in darkness and day,
   The drover boy trudges along ;
With Duty to guide him, he cheers the lone way
   With a whistle, a shout, or a song :
He laughs in the sunshine, he fears not the storm,
   He's familiar with hail, rain, and snow ;
For a hedgerow will shelter, a trot keep him warm,
   And his hat shade the sun from his brow.

     Then, heigh ! for the drover,
     The wide world all over,
       And, heigh ! for the bold drover boy.

There's a rare cunning look in the jolly dog's eye,
   Health and freedom in every limb ;
And each towering hill, reaching up to the sky,
   Is crowned with a trophy for him :

When the lights die away, he's the king of the road,
　Though his crown is as ragged as he,
An old black felt hat, with a brim slouched and broad,
　And his sceptre the stem of a tree.

　　Then, heigh! for the drover,
　　The wide world all over,
　　　And, heigh! for the bold drover boy.

DEAR ANNIE, FORGIVE ME.

I.

" Dear Annie, forgive me, I'm nigh broken-hearted,
   To think my fond love should have led you astray ;
It were better by far had some base falsehood started
   The love-links that bound us for many a day :
All my hopes in the future I'd freely surrender,
Could I but restore you to wealth, home, and splendour,
So artless, so loving, so young, and so tender,
   How sorely I've wronged you, no mortal can tell."

II.

" Dear husband," she cried, " I have no cause to blame you,
   Unsought, I determined my kindred to flee ;
No more let this home with its barrenness shame you,
   No palace on earth could be dearer to me :

Too long had I wasted the strength heaven gave me.
Sorely tempted by Sloth, who had sworn t' enslave me,
Heaven sent you, dear husband, to succour and save me,
    Regret ne'er shall lodge in this bosom of mine."

III.

" Heaven bless you, my darling, a truce to all sorrow,
    Hope's flickering lamp has rekindled once more ;
The cloud of misfortune that frowns on the morrow,
    Shall find me as firm as the rock on the shore :
This arm shall win strength from the beauty it pillows,
No more shall my spirit, love, droop like the willows,
But, scathless and free, in the midst of Fate's billows,
    Thy wishes shall guide me wherever I go."

IN THE YOUTH OF THE WORLD.

I.

In the youth of the world, ere man passed his childhood,
When oceans were shipless, and lands were untrod,
'Twas the toiler that conquered the desert and wildwood,
And cut the broad pathway to freedom and God.
While there's light in the heavens and hope in the morrow,
The proud soul of Labour, unshackled and strong,
Shall look up to its God from the headland and furrow,
And ask for new courage to strangle the wrong.

II.

In the dim factory light, in the depths of earth's bosom,
In workshop and storehouse, in garret and stall,
The old tree of knowledge, now budding, shall blossom,
And bend with delight for the comfort of all.
Then away with despair; through the dark clouds above us
A faint streak of light glimmers over us now,—
'Tis the beam of God's eye, bidding tyrants to love us,
And chasing the shadows that linger below.

WITH MEASURED TREAD THE SOWER WALKS.

I.

With measured tread the sower walks
    Across the furrowed land ;
From right to left, from left to right,
    He guides his brawny hand.
The seedlip hanging by his side,
    With choicest corn o'erflows,
A robin follows in his wake,
    And whistles as he sows.

II.

When Spring shall call her muster-roll
    Of legions sprung from toil,
And armies wave their emerald flags
    Triumphant o'er the soil—
A countless host with countless spears,
    Shall muster on the land,
For every grasp of golden grain
    That quits the sower's hand.

A HARVEST CHANT.

I.

THERE is no scene I love like the rich harvest field
  With its golden sheaves ranged in a row ;
For it tells a rare tale of ripe flagons of ale,
  And the triumph of sickle and plough.
And where is the music that equals the shout
  Of the farmer and peasant combined,
As the creaking old wain, bears the last load of grain,
  To be sheltered from shower and wind ?

II.

You remind me of woods, and the rich song of birds,
  Of the meadows and musical bees,
Of the worshipful choir, and tapering spire,
  That points up to heaven through the trees.
But, again will I sing, there is no scene on earth
  Like the field with the labourer's reward ;
And no music to me comes from flower or tree,
  Like the harvest shout raised to the Lord.

CLEAR AS CRYSTAL FLOWS THE COLNE.

I.

Rolling calmly through the meadows,
   Scarce a ripple stirs its breast ;
Now and then a few dim shadows
   Shoot across from East to West :
Such is still my native river,
   As it runs its course alone ;
Calmly, smooth, unruffled ever,
   Clear as crystal flows the Colne.

II.

Honoured friends, long cherished neighbours,
   As Fate calls you one by one,
May you calmly end your labours
   By the margin of the Colne :
Like your own, my native river,
   Till the sea demands its toll,
May the stream of life for ever
   Flow unruffled to its goal.

MY GRANDFATHER'S STORY.

I.

FAIRLY crusted with mould, in an old oaken chest,
   I discovered my grandfather's story;
Stirring deeds, pregnant truths, in strong language expressed,
   Give the relic a title to glory;
'Tis an unvarnished tale of an honest old man,
   Who disdained the false glitter of fashion,
And befriended a deed, or discarded a plan,
   Like a judge, without favour or passion.

But I cannot repeat all the tale in a song,
   Though each lesson I learned well and thorough;
But there's one, "Shun temptation to vice while you're young,
   And repentance will shun you to-morrow."

II.

'Tis a solemn old chest, built of sound English oak,
   Which a stout well-tanned hide doth environ;
Not a nail quits its hold, not a panel is broke,
   With stout hinges of sinewy iron:

Firm and true, like the man, and defying the rogue,
  With its ponderous padlock grown rusty,
That my grandfather named from a favourite dog
  He worthily christened " Old Trusty."

But I cannot repeat all the tale in a song,
  Though each lesson I learned well and thorough ;
But there's one, " Learn to labour when healthy and young,
  For disease may prostrate you to-morrow."

III.

There was naught in the chest when my grandfather died,
  Save the story I prize beyond measure ;
And the face of a cherry-cheeked English bride,
  My grandmother, grandfather's treasure :
Though it is but a shade in a worm-eaten frame,
  And a story of honest endeavour,
I would deem it a wrong to an honest man's name
  If I did not preserve them for ever.

But I cannot repeat all the tale in a song,
  Though each lesson I learned well and thorough,
But there's one, "Speak your mind to the weak and the
      strong,
  And they'll learn to respect you to-morrow."

IN MEMORIAM.

"Be mine," said Friendship, to her favourite son :

"I will," he cried, and placed her armour on.

"Not wholly thine," cried Love, in mournful guise ;

I claim the worship of the good and wise."

A beauteous pair, yclept Charity and Truth,

Then jointly sought, and thus addressed the youth :

"Hast thou forgotten that, in times long passed,

Thou said'st thou'd serve us truly to the last ?"

"I'll aid ye all !" the youth exclaimed, in glee,

And took the badge, "I SERVE," on bended knee.

How well he kept the promise he had given,

Is known on earth, and registered in heaven.

SOLITARY MUSING.

If thou wouldst think, straight quit the busy street,
For lonely spots suggest the richer thought.
It seems as though an essence from the dead
Renewed the vigour of the flagging brain,
And new life came from whence all life had flown,
And tongues long quiet learnt to speak again.
Such living thoughts arising from the grave
Are richer from the contrast of their birth.

ELEGIAC STANZAS.

Could Love have stayed thee, thou hadst never fled,
  Could Grief recal thee, surely thou would'st come,
For who could count the tears that we have shed,
  Or know the joy that filled our happy home?
Weeping, we saw thy slow, slow breath depart,
  And vainly asked of heaven a short respite;
Then felt a coldness gather round the heart,
  And saw the mid-day change to blackest night.
The light, the love, the wealth of this robbed home,
  With her departed; and, to us, it seems
A midnight 'neath a moonless, starless dome,
  Where all our thoughts are but the wildest dreams.
Those winning tones that ever bade him stay
  Will never greet the welcomed guest again:
The angel of our home has passed away,
  And naught but memoried goodness doth remain.

JUDGE NOT A MAN.

I.

Judge not a man by the cost of his clothing,
  Unheeding the life-path that he may pursue ;
Or oft you'll admire a heart that needs loathing,
  And fail to give honour where honour is due.
The palm may be hard and the fingers stiff-jointed,
  The coat may be tattered, the face worn with tears,
But greater than kings are Labour's anointed ;
  You can't judge a man by the coat that he wears

II.

Give me the man as a friend and a neighbour
  Who toils at the loom, at the spade or the plough,
Who wins his diploma of manhood by labour,
  And purchases wealth by the sweat of his brow.
Why should the broad-cloth alone be respected,
  And the man be despised who in fustian appears ?
The angels in heaven have their limbs unprotected ;
  You can't judge a man by the coat that he wears.

III.

Judge of a man by the work he is doing,

   Speak of a man as his actions demand;

Watch well the path that each is pursuing,

   And let the most worthy be chief o' the land!

And the man shall be found 'mid the close ranks of labour,

   Be known by the work that his industry rears,

And his chiefdom when won shall be dear to his neighbour:

   And we'll honour the man whatever he wears.

FREEDOM'S DAY.

I.

THE slave who wore his fetters without hope,
   The fool who spent a lifetime in complaining,
The king, the upstart, the tyrant, and the pope,
   Have died, as knaves and cowards die, defaming.
The labour of our lives has worked their woe,
   And those who scorned us perished 'mid our laughter,
For Truth was crowned on that immortal day
   To rule the world with Justice ever after.

II.

The age has passed when tyrants reigned supreme,
   And fattened on the misery they created;
The creed is dead that called the truth a dream,
   Whose dawn a thousand dead men long awaited.
The labour of our lives, and martyrs dead,
   Have purchased for the future peace and glory,
And how we fought on that immortal day,
   Shall be the theme of future song and story.

THERE'S PLENTY FOR ALL.

I.

THERE's plenty for all, but we thwart one another,
    And the weak gather weeds, while the strong cull the
        flowers
Let man aye treat man as a friend and a brother
   And there's plenty for all in this rich world of ours.
Had the Godhead been selfish, no frail flower blooming,
    Would, dying, bequeath its perfume to the air ;
And the life-giving streams, through our wide valleys roam-
        ing,
    Would have ne'er spread their circles, nor mirrored a
        star.

II.

Dark deeds and rare virtues, self-love and negation,
   In the wisest of natures have, struggling, met ;
And the page that records the good deeds of the nation,
   Is polluted with crimes that we fain would forget :

Did men love one another as firm as they hated,
    This world were a spot wherein no man could grieve ;
Will the palate of Woe with man's tears ne'er be sated ?
    Will man never practice to live and let live ?

III.

Shall the shadows of darkness grow shorter or longer ?
    Have martyrs unbowed trod the scaffold in vain ?
Will brotherly love become weaker or stronger ?
    The crimes of the past be enacted again ?
Fair Plenty shall enter the cottager's dwelling,
    Laughter will shake his fat sides at his board,
Pæans to Joy fill the breeze proudly swelling,
    And the wand of Old Time change the serf to a lord.

IN THE LONG DREARY WINTER.

I.

In the long dreary winter of querulous age,
  When the lights into shadows have blended,
And the glories of youth, with its vain equipage,
  Like the reign of a butterfly's ended,
May the old-fashioned type upon Memory's page
  Still recal from among those departed,
One friendship, unchilled by the winter of age,
  One love that Old Time has not thwarted.

II.

We seldom win friends in the winter of life,
  Age's chilliness seems to alarm us;
So, we'll pick up a few from the world's rugged strife,
  While youth casts a halo to warm us:
We can choose, if we will, as we journey along,
  For the friendless are aye melancholy;
And one, if no more, that we choose from the throng
  Shall help to make life's winter jolly.

WATERLOO.

I.

No BED of roses waits Napoleon,
  Though Paris greet him with her wanton charms:
Distraction meets him as he mounts the throne,
  For Europe rings with wild and vague alarms,
  And loud-mouthed tocsin calls the world to arms.
Each nation that has wept a sea of tears,
  With choked revenge and stifled anger warms,
  And high the flag of retribution rears
To wave its crimson folds above a sea of spears.

II.

The outlook may be dark, but he was born
  To look on danger with unshaken nerves,
And hence the gathering host is held in scorn.
  He little does who from his purpose swerves,
  And lackey plays to Time; but whom Time serves,
Will live to do, and though perchance he fail,
  Kind memory still his name and fame preserves,
  And chroniclers will live to tell the tale,
And show what stubborn rocks man's courage dare assail.

III.

On Belgium's plains a motley host have met.
Unknown to discipline, untrained to war;
The curse of Babel lingers with them yet,
But England bids great Wellington prepare
To be their mentor, trust, and guiding star;
For who but he can such disciples mould,
That History, forgetting what they were,
Believes them sprung from heroes stark and cold,
And trained to burning arms in battles manifold.

IV.

At length our chief receives the welcome words,
"Strange bivouac fires are burning at Beaumont."
Prepare ye now to hear the clash of swords,
The heartfelt curses of the baffled throng,
The crash of cannon, as it sweeps along,
The mingled noises of the waggon train,
The withering volley, like a mine upsprung,
The piercing shriek that swells the awful strain,
And tells the fearful cost of War's terrific reign.

V.

The fiercely raging thirst for human blood
Burns fiercer still at close of Quartre Bras ;
And what though Ligney has for hours withstood
The rush of valour and the heat of war,
A field more terrible and bloodier far
Alone can slake th' unconquerable thirst.
Look ye your last on yon pale evening star ;
To-morrow every hope that ye have nursed
May, like those gathered clouds, be scattered and dispersed.

VI.

Sleep ! warrior, sleep ! and bid the moon farewell,
Whose watery beams scarce reach the open plain ;
To-morrow, ere it burst o'er hill and dell,
Thy stiffened corse may rest among the slain.
Sleep, if thou canst, midst thunder, wind, and rain,
And hoard thy precious strength as though 'twere gold,
Forget the tempest for the hurricane.
If thou must dream, dream of those warriors old
Whose deeds are prone to rouse and stimulate the bold.

VII.

The Sabbath dawns without its quietude,
 And those calm tones that float upon its air,
 And say to all Earth's teeming multitude,
"Go to thy temple with a soul sincere,
 This day thy Lord allotted unto prayer,"
Are in the din of preparation lost.
 Above, around, unceasing everywhere,
 A buzzing noise comes from th' awak'ning host,
Like distant waters dashed upon a rock-bound coast.

VIII.

All is prepared: the skirmishers advance—
 Those pioneers of every bloody fray,
 And Jerome heads the panting troops of France,
While British heroes calmly stand at bay,
Now, let Imagination have full sway,
 And by her aid the assisted eye shall see
Those valiant warring men of France give way,
 Before the blaze of British musketry;
The first wave has recoiled t' advance more furiously.

IX.

The brunt of battle falls on Hugomont,
A simple homestead in a sea of corn ;
Brave hearts alone can make its weakness strong,
Alone can meet those withering shocks with scorn ;
They come to go—they go but to return ;
Save those whom Death has met upon the track,
And those whose limbs, by savage carnage torn,
Refuse to bear their mortal burthens back.
Alas ! their songs no more will cheer the bivouac.

X.

" Now rouse thee ! gallant Ney, thy turn has come :
Brave victor of a hundred fights, lead on ;
Be swift, be sure ; and fail not to strike home,
And glory waits thee," cried Napoleon.
Could mortal man interrogate the sun,
That eye of Heaven o'erlooking all below,
'Twould say—" The brave who fought at Marathon
Must aye the palm of victory allow
To those who fought and bled at famous Waterloo."

XI.

The trumpet sounds to glory or to death,
The air is rent with "Live the Emperor!"
Ten thousand swords are flashing from the sheath,
The tramp of men, the cannons' ceaseless roar,
The shriek of those who welter in their gore,
All, all, proclaim the culminating strife
That fools admire and wise men but deplore.
Oh! God! how cheap each hero holds his life,
Forgetful of the claims of mother, child, and wife!

XII.

The storm is gathering round thy roof, La Haye,
Oh! such a storm as thou hast never seen:
See, terror-stricken Nassau-men give way,
While swift-winged fear has pierced thy coats of green.
The burly Briton clings to thy demesne
As though it was the spot that gave him birth;
Thy shattered walls afford but half a screen,
Still, still, he swears to guard thy humble hearth,
Till life, at Honour's call, is swallowed up in death.

XIII.

Come, Picton, with thy braves of Quartro Bras,
A road scarce parts thee from the Gallic foe,
'Tis thou alone can stem the tide of war,
On thee depends a nation's weal or woe.
The eagle circling on its prey below,
The tiger crouching in its hidden lair,
Like thee, securely meditates the blow.
And what, though sad misfortune's been thy share,
There's not a break or strain thy courage can't repair.

XIV.

The magic words have passed from out thy lips,
",Deploy and fire!"   Oh! hear ye not the knell?
Behold how glory suffers an eclipse—
'Twas here, amid the fray, brave Picton fell,
His dying words re-echoing through the dell,
"Charge! charge! hurrah!" "Hurrah!" the echo said,
And ere the words from soft-winged zephyrs fell,
The spirit of the brave in haste had fled,
And Picton, gallant Picton, rested with the dead!

XV.

A wondrous clatter's heard throughout the fray,
Like that which cyclops make when anvils jar ;
With rapid strokes our cavalry belay
The steel-wrought breast-plate of the cuirassier,
Old Scotia's infantry, with limbs nigh bare,
Have ever cased their hearts in bravery ;
Behold them, how they prosper in the war !
" Scotland for ever ! " Hear ye not the cry
That bids the sternest foe to beat retreat or die ?

XVI.

Thus victory on victory is won ;
But who shall count the large and wond'rous cost ?
The blade of Ponsonby gleams in the sun,
And now, alas ! brave Ponsonby is lost !
Too far they follow the retreating host.
Mourn ! Britain, mourn, thy stricken heroes mourn !
Whose dauntless deeds of daring was thy boast ;
They treated danger as a thing of scorn,
And died for honour's sake as men to honour born.

XVII.

Now rouse thee, France, with all thy chivalry,
The game is desperate and the day nigh spent ;
The stubborn foe has long refused to fly—
Nay, jeered thee in his wanton merriment ;
Thy well-served guns have long and vainly rent
His ranks asunder—every gap has closed ;
A storm-torn cloud in yonder firmament,
That for a moment left the Heavens disclosed,
Does not more quickly heal, nor seem less discomposed.

XVIII.

Napoleon calls his old and trusty guard,
Whose deeds have crowned them with a dazzling fame ;
They ask for naught but glory for reward,
And hold defeat another word for shame.
His words are met with shouts of loud acclaim,
Like hounds in leash they long to join the sport ;
Oh ! what save death can their wild ardour tame ?
To serve Napoleon is the only thought
That animates their souls and prompts the fierce assault.

XIX.

Stand firm, ye Britons, on the storm-lashed crest;
Oh, heed ye not the loud and rallying drum?
Your courage now must bide a sterner test;
The braves of Jena and of Wagram come,
And they at least, will fail not to strike home.
Now, British hearts, let glory crown the day,
A well-earned laurel or a hero's tomb;
Lie still; ye've stood the storm from morn's first ray,
Till roused to see the surge of stern despair give way.

XX.

From right to left th' Imperial troops advance,
With lusty shouts and banners poised in air;
The bayonets glitter and the red plumes dance,
The Prussians press upon their right and rear.
Oh! can it be that he is held in fear
Whose ears were pampered by the clash of swords,
Whose eyes glanced brighter at the glittering spear?
Alas! alas! he breathes the fatal words,
"Now lead on, Gallant Ney!" and quits his warlike hordes.

XXI.

Gainst either flank a raging storm prevails,
And shot and shell incessantly are plied ;
The storms of other wars were squeamish gales
To that which gathers with the rushing tide.
The powers of Hell, to mortal men allied,
Seem bent on sweeping mankind from the field ;
Or, is it Heaven, in anger at man's pride,
That lends destruction to the arms they wield,
And tears their soul with rage, that they may sooner yield ?

XXII.

A withering volley strikes the foremost rank,
And heroes quail who never quailed before !
A galling fire now opens on each flank,
And thousands welter in their crimson gore.
Now, Wellington, that mighty god of war,
With eagle's eye detects the foe's mischance ;
He bids his guards " Be ready and prepare !"
Himself directs his eager troops' advance,
And scattered to the winds the mighty power of France.

XXIII.

Now, ply your shuttles, weavers of the night,
And hide from every eye this scene of woe;
Stay, stay the gory hand of fierce delight,
That deals destruction on a fallen foe;
Enough, enough, is that sad overthrow,
It makes amends for every former wrong;
With Pity's tears my anguished eyes o'erflow;
I love to see kind Mercy rule the strong,
And deem that fell revenge to cowards doth belong.

———

JOY EVERYWHERE.

_____

I.

Who dares to assert that no joy's to be found?
  There is no place without it, I trow;
It falls from the sky, it springs from the ground,
  I can find it wherever I go.
In the bush, in the brake, in the forest and fen,
  On mountain, on moorland and plain,
In my lone little cot in the heart of the glen,
  In my boat, as she rides o'er the main.
      So, look for Joy steadily, search for it readily,
        Find it, and make it your friend.

II.

'Tis not wedded to creed, to climate, or kind,
  You may find it wherever you're whirled;
And I've seen it ere now, through eyelids quite blind,
  Look laughingly out on the world:

I've seen it, where Winter ruled all the year round,
　　Where the splendour of Summer ne'er set,
And I've known it to burst through the stoniest ground,
　　In the midst of despair and regret.
　　　　So, look for Joy steadily, search for it readily.
　　　　Find it, and make it your friend.

III.

I tell you that Joy is a free-handed friend,
　　And cares not for station or gold ;
To the highest 'twill reach, to the lowest 'twill bend,
　　And never betray young or old :
It will light up the furrows on Age's torn brow,
　　And brighten its blear eyes with pride ;
On the smooth cheek of Youth it will redden and glow
　　And quicken the life-giving tide.
　　　　So, look for Joy steadily, search for it readily,
　　　　Find it, and make it your friend.

CEASE NOT TO TOIL.

I.

Cease not to toil, although thou hast treasure—
   He who spurns labour should never be fed;
The man whose existence is made up of pleasure
   Has no claim to the feast that King Labour has spread.
He's a poor useless drone who ne'er wrought for his living,
   Although he have health, wealth, and strength at command;
A pauper the toiler is ever relieving,
   A blot on earth's surface—a weed in the land.

There's nothing we gaze at with awe and with wonder,
   There's nothing wherein grace and beauty can blend,
From the arched sky above to the great globe that's under,
   But labour's its parent, protector, and friend.

III.

To win and to wear is the law of our nature—
    The toil of the winning enhancing the prize ;
A law never altered, but binding each creature,
    The great and the little, the foolish, the wise.
As ages roll onward, the toiler, uplifted,
    Shall blush every idler with merited shame ;
No more shall the gains of his labour be sifted,
    While glory encircles his world-worshipped name.

    There's nothing we gaze at with awe and with wonder,
        There's nothing wherein grace and beauty can blend,
    From the arched sky above to the great globe that's under,
        But labour's its parent, protector, and friend.

EVENING, SWEET EVENING.

I.

The rich-jewelled morn may be bounteous of health,
  But Evening, sweet Evening, for me,
When I stroll with my love by the fair winding Dove,
  And the stars crown each tower and tree.
The crimson-faced day and the high sultry noon,
  I envy not those who can prize,
For I covet them not, earth is one golden spot,
  In the light of my love's deep blue eyes.

II.

The rich-jewelled morn and the crimson-faced day,
  In whose glare craft and treachery move,
Must give way to the night, whose soft mellowed light
  Is the friend and promoter of love.
What to me are the glories of daylight, I ask,
  If my love is not free from control?
There is nought but despair, cruel torments, and care
  When I miss the sweet maid of my soul.

LONDON:

PRINTED BY THE WESTMINSTER PRINTING COMPANY,
132, DRURY LANE, W.C.